SKIN DEEP

SKIN DEEP

MAN'S APPOINTMENT WITH DESTINY

A NOVEL BY

LINDA SARGENT

WinePress Publishing (PO Box 428, Enumclaw, WA 98022) functions only as book publisher. As such, the ultimate design, content, editorial accuracy, and views expressed or implied in this work are those of the author.

Unless otherwise noted, all Scriptures are taken from the King James Version of the Bible.

ISBN 1-57921-856-3
Library of Congress Catalog Card Number: 2006902889

To Louis, Lila, Jim, Andrew,
Sarah, and, of course, Hailey

Acknowledgments

The author gratefully acknowledges the following people who helped make this novel possible:

My husband, Jim, for his constant encouragement for me to finish this project and for covering my appointments, obligations, responsibilities, and work schedule for the last seven months so that I could;

My son, Andrew, whose insight into the unique date of June 6, 2006 sparked the idea to write this novel. Also, thanks for helping with some of the outlines;

My daughter, Sarah, who sacrificed her time to step in and carry me during a time when I was completely overwhelmed;

My parents who raised me in a Christian home and continually encouraged me to pursue life with a can-do attitude. They told me one day I'd thank them. Mom and Dad, I thank you;

Dr. Dennis E. Hensley for his enthusiasm and support for this project and for all of his assistance with the editing, proofreading, and positive suggestions for improvement. You're the best;

My friend, Irvin Baxter, our trumpet on the wall, for his uncompromised and tireless dedication to serve the Body of Christ and fulfill the will of God.

Introduction

And he causeth all, both small and great, rich and poor,
free and bond, to receive a mark in their right hand,
or in their foreheads:
And that no man might buy or sell,
save he that had the mark
or the name of the Beast, or the number of his name.
Here is wisdom. Let him that hath understanding count
the number of the Beast: for it is the number of a man;
and his number is Six hundred threescore and six.

The Revelation of Saint John The Divine
Chapter 13: 16–18

It is believed that the apostle John wrote the words of The Revelation while banished on the Island of Patmos, off the western coast of Asia Minor. The exact date is uncertain, but according to traditional opinion, it was circa A.D. 96.

Although John penned the words, he declared in Revelation 1:1 they were actually the revelation of Jesus Christ.

In the event that the Book of Revelation reveals future events, Chapter 13 warns of a time when all must take a number or mark in order to transact business. Could it be that John foretold of a national or even international identification number using an RFID chip or retinal scan? If so, how close are we to seeing the use of the mark or number of the Beast?

CHAPTER ONE

Hank Rollins had worked at Zipp Courier for forty years. He was only fifty-five the day he was murdered. He'd started as a part-time warehouse worker while still in high school, barely fourteen with a fake work permit. Hank was the oldest of five kids and realized even at that early age every buck was important. The family grew up in a modest, but clean, home in the Bronx. His mother worked two jobs to feed and clothe them and was away from the family more than not. No one seemed to know, or at least they weren't telling, where dad was.

Hank spent most of his childhood helping to rear the younger ones. He sometimes regretted that he didn't get to hang out with his friends or join clubs after school like the other boys. He knew that those weren't options for him, so he didn't bother to ask. He pretended it didn't matter, but his mother knew better; still, there just wasn't much she could do about it. Through it all, Hank learned a good work ethic but also some of life's lessons and disappointments at an early age. Hank wasn't bitter, just tired.

Now, at age fifty five, he was in mid-management at Zipp Courier. His branch office was located close to the East River on Front Street and was responsible for scheduling all the pickups and deliveries for offices, businesses, and banks in the financial district of lower Manhattan. He oversaw a fleet of fifteen armored vehicles and forty-five trained security guards, three to each vehicle. Each day began with an equipment and weapons check and a rundown of the day's schedule. Hank mapped out different routes for the drivers so that each day was varied enough to throw off anyone trying to discern a pattern and set up an easy heist.

This day began like any other. The drivers and guards reported at the usual time, ready for their assignments. This summer was predicted to be a record breaker in several categories—early hurricanes, floods in the South, drought in the North and West, but, worst of all, record heat.

Whenever possible, Hank tried to get most of the day's heavy jobs scheduled before noon to avoid the oppressive afternoon heat. Summer had arrived before the calendar said it should, and the thermostat outside Hank's window was already creeping in the mid-eighties by 8:00 A.M. Hank had been in his office for a couple of hours going over the orders and the daily schedules and mapping out the routes for the early pickups.

Mondays were always the worst. Tourists were everywhere, all eager to get an early start on all the sightseeing; grumpy commuters were still tired from the prior week; fresh produce truck drivers were trying to get a jump on deliveries to the area restaurants and markets; merchants were gearing up for a new week. The hoards were reluctantly returning to another work week. But not Hank; at least not this Monday. He'd been anticipating this day ever since he had gotten the unusual telephone call two weeks ago.

"Hello, Mr. Rollins," the voice began.

Hank paused before he spoke, but the voice continued.

"You don't know me. We've never actually met, but I've done an extensive background check on you and your business. I have a proposition that I believe you'll find interesting. One that could hasten your retirement."

Hank thought he vaguely recognized the voice for a second and interrupted.

"Is that you, Carl?" Hank asked. "What are you talking about? You been drinking again?" Hank and Carl had been friends since high school. They'd met almost on the first day of their junior year while hanging out in the parking lot in back of the school, smoking cigarettes before making their way into class. They'd thought they were pretty cool as they lit up and watched the jocks trying to flirt with the cheerleaders or the nerds chatting it up with each other about some homework assignment. Early in the school year, Hank and Carl had been in detention together, more than once, for smoking in the boy's locker room, and they'd both done time in juvenile detention for truancy and underage drinking.

After Hank's second arrest, his mother stepped in and convincingly reminded Hank that he'd been taught better than that, and his behavior wouldn't be tolerated. Hank realized he'd never get out of poverty and get ahead if he didn't finish high school and stay out of trouble. So, he started taking more of an interest in his classes and less in the parking lot activities. He graduated on time. He was the smarter of the two friends and after high school took a few courses in mechanics and management skills with the help of a tuition scholarship at a local career center.

Carl eventually dropped out of school after he couldn't pass the eleventh grade. It was hard for him to find a job, even harder for him to keep it. But, through it all, Hank and Carl remained friends, were each other's best men at their weddings, and saw each other as often as possible.

Carl still liked his booze and usually hit it hard on the weekends. He was always playing some practical joke, trying to pull a fast one on Hank. Hank played along most of the time and let Carl think he'd tricked him. They usually got a good laugh out of it, and Carl's jokes sometimes eased the boredom of Hank's daily routine as well.

"This isn't Carl, Mr. Rollins."

The voice sounded serious and had a slight accent. It was deliberate and resolute. And, Carl never called Hank "Mr. Rollins," even as a joke. *No, it definitely wasn't Carl,* Hank thought, and quickly adjusted to a more business response.

"Excuse me sir, how may I help you?" Hank asked, this time in a more appropriate manner.

"I'd like to speak to you about a business transaction, maybe employ your services, but not over the phone. I'll stop by at the close of today's business, if you're interested," the voice answered.

"Uh, sure, this afternoon will be just fine. But who are you? What do you look like?"

But there was no answer, just dead air, and then a click.

At exactly 6:10 P.M., after all of the drivers had gone home for the day, a mysterious man whose voice matched the caller's stepped inside Hank's office. The man was dressed in a nice suit and tie, and he looked like he was just another executive in town for a Monday morning meeting, power lunch and a return flight on the corporate jet, home in time for dinner. As soon as Hank closed his office door, the stranger began.

"Mr. Rollins, as I said earlier, my people have done some checking on Zipp Courier. We know that you've spent forty years with the company and have climbed your way up through management. That's all very admirable, but . . . we believe that you've probably had enough of it all, and if only you had the money, you'd like to retire and buy a small place for you and your wife in rural Vermont. Wanda is as tired as you after rearing the four children and trying to make ends meet on your modest salary. She'd like to spend more time in the garden and maybe only work part time."

As the stranger spoke, Hank tried to stay focused. *How did this man know so much about him, his wife, their dreams, and how long he'd been with Zipp? And who was the "we" he kept referring to?*

"Look, mister . . .?" Hank paused and waited for the stranger to supply the missing name. When he didn't, Hank finally spoke up. "You know a lot about me. How about telling me something about yourself, 'your people,' as you call them? For starters, what's your name?"

The stranger responded slowly but deliberately. "Names aren't important. There's a time for everything, and when the time is right, you'll be given information. For right now, you just need to listen carefully. If you're not interested in my proposal, I'll leave. Either way, it would be in your best interest if you took the position that this conversation never took place." He locked eyes with Hank But, he already knew that Hank wouldn't ask him to leave.

The stranger talked on and on about other details of Hank's life and the business operations. It was obvious that he knew a lot about both. He knew that Hank's whole life had been routine—doing the expected, no risks, no adventures. Every day, every week, every month, completely predictable. Until today. And today, here was a total stranger, completely unexpected, sitting across from Hank, offering early retirement. *Why?*

Hank listened politely, nodded when he thought he was supposed to, and realized his life had been pretty uneventful. He'd never strayed from the law since he was a kid in high school. He got up and went to work at the same time each day and came home right after work at the same time and by the same route each night. He and Wanda had taken a few days of vacation each year and driven to the beach with the kids when they were younger. On weekends they usually rented a movie or had the neighbors over for a backyard cookout; nothing fancy and certainly nothing out of the ordinary.

Even after all of the children left home, Hank and Wanda never changed their routines, never splurged on a thing. This stranger's visit was the only unexpected event in Hank's life for as long as he could remember. Maybe that's why his curiosity finally got the best of him

"OK, I'll bite. How can I help you? But, first I'm curious, why have you taken such an interest in me and the wife? How do you know so much about us?"

"One step at a time, Mr. Rollins," the voice replied. "And I will ask the questions, are we clear?"

What was Hank supposed to say? The stranger then continued, a little annoyed that Hank had demanded any information.

"On Monday, June 6, someone from Global Financial Bank's headquarters over on Wall Street will call to hire Zipp Courier to pick up and transfer some computer tapes to a credit bureau on West Thames Street for storage. My, shall we say, 'associates' are interested in intercepting the transfer, and they will pay handsomely to do so. In the neighborhood of $1.2 million."

The stranger never flinched, never took his eyes off Hank. He spoke as though he'd made this type of offer every day. Hank tried to remain calm, to breathe normally, to appear as though he'd had this type of offer every day, although the stranger knew otherwise. Hank studied the stranger. Questions raced through his mind as he tried to process the stranger's statements. *What could be on a computer tape worth $1.2 million? If the information was that valuable, why was it going to storage? What did the stranger and, 'his associates,' want with the tapes? Was this conversation being recorded? What were the risks? There had to be risks. What would happen to Hank if he got caught? More importantly, what would he tell Wanda?*

These were questions he was sure the stranger wouldn't answer anymore than he'd tell Hank his name. In the calmest voice he could manage, Hank replied, "I suppose you have worked out all the details, no mistakes, no loose ends." It was more of a question than an assumption. Hank needed all the assurance he could get.

"We have."

"So, how can I be sure this can't be traced back to me?" Hank asked.

"Once the delivery has been procured and in our possession your money will be wired to an off shore untraceable account. You should give the appearance that you are making every effort to trace the loss. Your company's reputation for using enhanced safety procedures and its history of success will go a long way to help this appear as just a random mishap. You will stay at your job a few more months, let the dust settle, then announce your retirement. Tell your supervisor you've put in forty years, your wife's health is not so good, and you want to slow down, and enjoy what's left of your life."

The stranger paused and then leaned forward, closer to Hank as he continued, "I'm sure you realize that it would be foolish for you to purchase any big ticket items or do anything to call attention to yourself."

He hesitated again, to give special emphasis to his next statement. In a lowered his voice he measured his words and slowly said, "And, as you might guess, my associates and I demand discretion and secrecy. No one is to know about this, including Wanda, or the deal's off. We walk away and you don't get your money. Do you understand?

"Yeah . . ., of course," Hank quickly replied but wondered how he would ever keep it from Wanda.

"So, do we have a deal?" The stranger asked.

Hank stared at the stranger, trying but failing to read his face and voice for any clue as to why this delivery was such a prize, why they had picked him. But then, the answer most likely wasn't on Hank's need to know list. He didn't want to appear too eager and didn't want the guy to think he could just walk in, throw around some money and Hank would be willing to sell his soul. But this was the big break he'd waited for his whole life. He and Wanda would be on easy street. They could just disappear into the countryside. They didn't need anything fancy. A slower pace and quiet sunsets would be reward enough for them.

The questions running through his mind wouldn't stop, and he could feel his conscience pressing in. But, without taking his eyes off of the stranger sitting across from him Hank said, "Well, mister . . ., I will tell you, that as of right now, no one from Global Financial Bank has hired Zipp to do anything. If they do, I can and will juggle some things around to get it scheduled. And, if someone does happen to call, as you say they will, I believe we can work out something to get the transport from Global Financial to another pick up point for your associates without calling attention to it."

There, he'd done it and without one stutter or hesitation. Hank was nervous, but he wasn't about to let the stranger know it. He could feel a light sweat beginning to form on the back of his neck and his forehead. He hoped the stranger wouldn't notice.

"Excellent, Mr. Rollins," the stranger responded. "I can assure you that someone will be calling. I know you will work out all the details, and I'll be in touch in a few days to check on your progress. In the meantime, I will arrange for your offshore account, as well as the other details of this transaction."

The stranger then rose, buttoned his suit coat, nodded at Hank, and walked out the door. Hank watched him climb into a waiting car and disappear around the corner.

Just as he promised, the stranger called, usually every two to three days, to check on Hank's progress with the routing plans. And, sure enough, two days after the stranger's visit, someone from Global Financial Bank called Zipp Courier to schedule a pick up of computer tapes to be delivered to the credit bureau on West Thames on June 6th. Hank took the call and set it up for the first thing that morning. He would personally supervise it himself.

For the next two weeks, Hank couldn't get the meeting with the stranger off of his mind. He replayed the conversation in his head at least a dozen times a day as he worked out a plan. He finally decided the boxes of tapes would be dropped off at the service garage, just behind the front office. There was a narrow alley between the buildings where Zipp's vans routinely came and went. Nothing would look suspicious or out of the ordinary. From there, as far as anyone else was concerned, someone from the credit bureau would pick up the containers. It was a small load, comparatively speaking, just seven boxes. Hank was sure that no one would notice. The drivers would all be out on jobs. He rehearsed the plan again in his mind and tried to foresee any possible hang-ups. He felt confident it would work. Hank dreamed of rural Vermont. He could not fail.

CHAPTER TWO

On the streets of New York City, in the seedy underworld of illegal commerce and trade, everyone knew three things about Vivo Solana: he was smart, well connected, and ruthless. They knew not to mistake his congenial smile as a sign of weakness or friendship. Solana was shrewd in his business dealings and no one got a second chance to double-cross him. Some might say he was just plain evil.

He hadn't always been that way. Vivo had once been a friend to everyone and known as, "Buddy," because he was. He had been brought up in a good home by two good parents with good values. They were immigrants from Spain, and "Buddy" sounded very American to them, much more than Vivo, the patriarch family name given to every first born male. They'd worked hard and told Buddy if he did also, he'd succeed. He was the first generation to have a formal education, and he was determined to fulfill his parents' dreams for him.

So, Buddy studied hard in school, played by the rules, and, at first, it seemed as though things would go just as his parents had predicted. He was a serious and dedicated student at City College of New York and completed his business degree in four years. His grades were above average, but nothing extraordinary, so he was grateful and relieved for the offer from Global Financial for a position in its trust department.

Buddy was a dedicated employee and a team player. He tried to make friends with everyone, even those outside his department. He especially like the guys in the security and receiving departments, although he didn't get to see them too often. He declined his colleagues' invitations to skip out early on Fridays to meet at the corner bar. Instead, he lived a disciplined life, worked overtime and took the ridicule in stride.

By the time he was thirty, his thick dark hair was peppered with gray on top and completely gray at the temples. It complemented his translucent light blue eyes and olive colored skin. He kept it short, but stylish. He was tall and lean with angular facial features, and he paid close attention to his appearance and grooming. Upon meeting Buddy Solana, he at first gave one the impression that he was sophisticated and on the fast track for an executive position at Global.

Although he was strikingly handsome, he lacked finesse and polish. He was loud and his mannerisms were awkward. His voice was too high and frequently cracked when he spoke. He oftentimes laughed uncontrollably at his own jokes that others thought were dull and boorish. Most of the time it was just plain uncomfortable to watch him in any social setting. Others were embarrassed for him even when he didn't realize just how foolish he looked. As long as he kept quiet, he made a good outward impression. That all changed as soon as he opened his mouth.

After several years, it was obvious that he'd never make it very far in the corporate arena, especially if it meant he'd have to deal more directly with the public. In the trust department, Buddy was out of sight most of the time. But, it was not the life he had dreamed of as the hard working child of immigrant parents.

He had tried to make it in the honest world. Buddy hid his disappointment when he was repeatedly passed over for promotions he knew he deserved based on performance. In his mind, he would hear his parents' encouragement, *work harder, Buddy, it'll come.* He vowed to stick it out for a few more years, hoping and expecting things to change. They didn't. Finally, he decided to take matters into his own hands.

The first thing he did was drop that silly nickname that was supposed to open doors and help him fit into Corporate America. Vivo had worked with some of the best business and financial minds in the banking industry at Global Financial, and he'd learned the operations inside and out. He had been given access to all of the customers' personal data, and through his friends in the receiving department, he had learned where the computer tapes with the information were stored, and that other large banks generally followed the same procedure. He also knew that one day his knowledge and experience would be valuable; if not to Global Financial and its board of directors, to someone else.

Without much notice or fanfare, Vivo left Global, cut all ties with his co-workers, and faded into obscurity. He'd saved enough money to live on for a few months so he could seclude himself into a life that wouldn't draw attention. After a few months, he set up a small brokerage firm under an assumed name, which served as a legitimate front for his real business: procuring and selling stolen personal information around the world.

His first strike was against a Virginia Department of Motor Vehicles office where his people rammed a vehicle through a back wall and drove off with files containing Social Security numbers and dates of birth of about eight thousand people. The information was quickly sold and distributed to one of Vivo's clients in Mexico City, who used it to obtain drivers' licenses for illegal immigrants smuggled across the border states. Once here, the foreigners were promised jobs so they could pay for their false identifications. Little did they know that after they were transported across the border to a remote place with a foreign language, where ties with home were severed, the cost of the stolen information doubled or tripled to a price they could never pay, and they became indentured servants to whomever had arranged to smuggle them into the country.

Vivo had successfully pulled off similar jobs at other state departments of motor vehicles, all of which increased his fortune and reputation for being a good source of valuable information. There was a big demand for legitimate personal data, and finding a buyer was never a problem. After several BMV heists, it was time to go to the next level; time to acquire customer bank files with enough personal information that a thief could access the owner's bank account or set up new ones under the stolen identity. Vivo knew exactly where he'd start—The Big Three in lower Manhattan.

CHAPTER THREE 

On June 6th, just as scheduled, at exactly 8:30 AM Zipp Courier's van backed up to the rear door of Global Financial. There were no armed guards accompanying the driver today, not just for a pickup of some computer tapes going to storage. At least that's what Hank told his driver. The driver got out, knocked on the door, and held up his credentials and photo identification to the 6" x 6" reinforced glass pane for the bank's security guard to examine. Seconds later, the double steel door clicked and opened.

The boxes were stacked and waiting, and it only took ten minutes to load them all into the van. After the driver signed the receipt, he jumped in and took off. Hank had instructed him to pick up the cargo and return it to the garage before going to his next job. Hank was always trying new time management techniques that he'd read about in *Business Weekly*. This was probably the latest tip to make every minute count, the driver thought. Hank assured him he'd take care of getting the boxes to their final destination.

Once the load was safely inside the garage and the driver was well on his way to his next job, Hank called the number he'd been given the day before during one of the stranger's calls. He could barely contain his anxiety. Sweat beads broke out on his forehead, and his breathing was rushed. This call would confirm the delivery and start the transfer of his funds. So far, everything had gone off like clockwork. *Could it really be this easy?* he wondered. After two rings, someone picked up the phone on the other end but said nothing.

"Hello, are you there?" Hank finally asked.

"Has the package arrived?" was the only reply Hank got. It was the stranger.

"Yes, the package is here," Hank answered.

"Good. I will make the call to start the wire transfer of the money. Within the half hour my associates will be over to pick up the boxes and provide you with information and instructions on how to access your account."

Less than thirty minutes later, a dark, late model unmarked van with tinted windows pulled around the corner and into the narrow drive between the buildings. Hank had covered the surveillance camera that scanned the area where the boxes were waiting as soon as the last driver pulled out thirty minutes earlier. Hank was waiting by the rear door as the van pulled in and was unable to see that its license plate was missing. It crawled to a stop next to where he pointed to the boxes, and the van's doors swung open simultaneously.

There were four men altogether, of average height, dressed in black pants, shirts and light weight blazers, with black caps covering most of their faces. The driver left the engine running and hurried to the back of the van and opened the double doors. Hank watched as the driver motioned with his hands toward the waiting cargo and spoke in muffled tones. The other three jumped in unison and followed the directions as he spoke.

Within less than two minutes the boxes were loaded. *Man, these guys were fast*, Hank thought and for a second wondered about offering them a regular job with Zipp. He quickly remembered he wouldn't be there much longer himself and just tried to concentrate on completing this job. Hank was nervous and eager for them to finish and be on their way before anyone could show up unexpectedly.

Once the boxes were loaded, the one who'd been giving all of the orders, approached Hank with an envelope. Hank momentarily looked at the man, and as their eyes met he felt a chill run through him. Looking back were the coldest, darkest eyes Hank had ever seen. They were like a shark's eyes—black and lifeless—an opening into an abyss. Not a word was spoken, just the split second glance.

As Hank reached for the envelope he briefly noticed the dark gloved hand draw a pistol from the man's left side of his coat, but Hank saw it too late to react or retreat to safety. Hank was defenseless; there was no place to hide in the narrow lane between the buildings. It all happened so fast, no one even noticed the small commotion or heard the muffled shots. Hank took two hits to the chest at close range. The shooter put his hand and arm around Hank's shoulder to break the fall. Hank managed to fix his eyes on the shooter and mouth the word, "Why?"

"Sorry, pal, I have my orders," the shooter replied as he laid him down by the door and grabbed the envelope before jumping into the waiting van. All of Zipp's drivers were long gone by now, so only Hank was there to cover the phones and dispatch. No one would return for at least a couple of hours.

The black van backed out of the side alley and left slowly and inconspicuously. It traveled south on Front Street and headed for Pier 11, where a Thunderbird Formula 25' PC was waiting to receive the stolen tapes. The stranger never really knew who was in charge of these jobs or where the boxes ultimately went. He just followed orders like all of the others. Discussion between the men other than instructions for getting the job done was strictly forbidden. Legitimate names were never exchanged.

No one even noticed the van leave except Hank, who was all alone now and still clinging to what little life he had left. On the ground next to the rear door, Hank just looked like another bundle, another early drop waiting to be delivered.

In his last seconds of life, Hank Rollins dimly sorted through the short day's events and the last two weeks since the stranger first contacted him. He knew he'd fallen for a trap and false flatteries. A get rich quick scam. *How stupid I was to believe such a lie.* The questions once again came to his mind but more slowly now. There were still no answers. He knew his time was short. He could feel his life fading as his body shut down. As he drew his last breath and felt the darkness come, Hank was still trying to figure out what could be on the computer tapes worth $1.2 million and a tired man's life.

CHAPTER FOUR

Hank's death was initially ruled another senseless homicide in New York City, perhaps a wanna-be gang member looking for an easy hit. As part of an initiation, at a minimum, most gangs required a new recruit to prove himself worthy of membership by committing a major crime. It could be armed robbery, rape, or murder, so long as the punk proved he was tough enough to hang with the seasoned hoodlums.

But, after a thorough investigation and after Global Financial Bank discovered that the computer tapes never made it to the credit bureau, the police determined Hank's murder was probably the result of a carefully timed and executed plan, and not a random homicide. Ten days later, the search for the missing boxes was suspended; there weren't any clues, no one on the street was talking, and the trail had gone cold.

The president and chairman of the board of Global Financial Bank called a meeting of the senior management team to review the extent of the loss and to devise a plan to address the negative publicity and to beef up security.

The public, and especially anyone affected, was uneasy and losing confidence in the metropolitan area banks. People wanted more definite answers to a problem that seemed to be escalating. A month earlier, One World Bank and International Bank of Commerce had issued apologies and assurances to their customers, because financial records were missing and suspected to have been stolen by bank employees or lost by storage bureaus (no one knew for sure). In all, almost a million customers' personal data were unaccounted for. With the information, a thief could gain access to any of the customers' accounts and withdraw money at will. Most of the thieves knew to strike quickly before the account owners were alerted and had a chance to change their personal identification numbers or close the account.

On the secondary market, the personal information was sold over and over to hundreds of individuals, who, in turn, used it to obtain phony passports, open charge card accounts or use existing ones, establish utility services and run up charges. The thieves usually had goods and services delivered to their own address, more often to a post office box, and the true owner wasn't tipped off for months. By then, hundreds, but more likely thousands of dollars had been fraudulently charged against the person's credit or stolen from his or her bank account.

To make matters worse, it could take years, if ever, to correct and restore the person's good name and credit. Apologies and assurances meant nothing to the victims. Global Financial Bank had to do more.

The corporate offices of Global Financial Bank occupied the top six floors of the bank's building in lower Manhattan. The board room was in a corner suite on the penthouse level and provided a panoramic view of New York City. On a clear day, one could pick out landmarks in eastern New Jersey.

The room was both impressive and intimidating. It featured custom made book shelves and cabinets, some of which displayed original bronze sculptures by Frederic Remington and Rodin. Lining the walls were oil portraits with brass name plates of former presidents and CEOs that hung as constant reminders that their ghosts were still present to hold each successor board of directors accountable. On one wall there was a dramatic marble and rich mahogany wood paneled fireplace in the center of two fifteen-foot-wide, ceiling to floor windows that faced south toward the Upper New York Bay.

A comfortable sitting area was arranged by the fireplace. Slight gold accents in the draperies and upholstered chairs complemented the numerous imported genuine Persian rugs throughout the room. Deep crown molding and carved panels in the ten-foot-high ceilings completed the architectural details. Indeed, it was a showplace.

But, the forty-foot-long conference table with burgundy leather side chairs under it in the center of the room was the true focal point. Decisions of the greatest magnitude were made around it.

The officers and senior management of the company, along with their support staff who were called to the meeting entered the room and took their places. The mood was somber. No one knew for sure exactly what had happened to the tapes, and no one wanted to call much attention to himself lest he be put in charge of the investigation. The whole thing was a mess and one wrong move or decision could cost someone his career.

There was a variety of different ideas presented of how to proceed and handle the situation. Some thought it best to lay low and not make an announcement right away, just wait and see if the missing tapes turned up. Others believed immediate action was necessary, and this was just the latest in a series of data losses and breaches similar to those that had forced the other local banks to warn their customers that personal information had been compromised.

And, this wasn't just happening to banks in Manhattan. There were more reports about stolen customer data occurring in other parts of the nation. But, in the cases where bank employees were involved with the theft, or the banks may have been careless with the storage or protection of the information, ultimately, the financial institution had to replace the money for their customers because of the breach. The banking industry was starting to take a heavy hit and something had to be done before it got out of hand.

President and CEO George Maxwell watched and listened. He was looking for leadership and accountability—someone to step up and show some guts. He also wanted as much information as possible from those in the room before he took over the meeting and announced his decision. After twenty minutes of listening to the others debate the issue, he rose from his place at the head of the conference table, held up his hand for silence, and waited for the room to become quiet.

"Thank you all for being here on such short notice. As you know, Global has taken a hit that could have enormous repercussions. I have listened to all of you and carefully considered your suggestions, even those with which I disagree.

I believe we must handle this with quick and decisive actions, and that Global Financial's customers must be notified immediately."

Maxwell's speech had become more assertive and less casual by now.

"This institution's founder, Morton Tarkington, and five generations of family control built Global Financial to where it is today by providing good services and information to our customers. From the beginning, the leaders of this bank emphasized the importance of treating everyone with honesty, and of being completely trustworthy. Although we've seen many changes in Global Financial, as well as the banking industry in general, these enduring values have remained the same."

Maxwell was slowly circling the table now as he spoke. He had taken control and was connecting with each one in the room by closing the distance between them. He stopped at the portrait of Mr. Tarkington before continuing.

"It may sound corny to us now sitting in this plush corporate board room, but Global Financial Bank was established nearly a century and a half ago with the reputation as, 'the safest safe in town.' It stood when other banks had failed during the frequent bank panics of the late 1800s and before the federal government created deposit insurance for banks." He turned and looked at the founder and momentarily paused before continuing.

"Our predecessors," he said with a slight wave toward Tarkington's portrait, "recognized the economic warning signs just before that bleak day in October, 1929, and wisely converted the investment portfolios into cash, and Global survived the resulting run on banks. Since that day, Global

Financial has enjoyed growth and has never lost sight of its history and traditions. It is synonymous with integrity. If we don't disclose this matter and word leaks out that we knew, our customers could lose all confidence in our leadership." Maxwell hesitated, then spoke with an urgency in his voice.

"As you know, we hold more than $740 billion in assets that belong to some of this world's wealthiest citizens and corporations. I would hate to see Global Financial lose any of its holdings, as would our shareholders." Maxwell emphasized those last words, in particular. "I will not allow Global's good name to be tarnished over this. The public is looking for leadership and answers. We need to let people know they can look to us to find it."

George Maxwell's command of the room was obvious. As he spoke, the room stilled and tensions eased. Heads nodded in agreement. He loved to recount the history of the bank and recall the early pioneers who had stood in the position he now enjoyed. No one stepped forward with any tangible ideas of how to confront the problem. George knew they were looking to him for direction and would stand behind him. As always, he had a plan and was confident it would succeed.

George Maxwell instructed one of his executive vice presidents to start working with the legal department on a rough draft of an announcement to the customers. The first draft was to be on his desk within twenty-four hours. Also, he wanted a complete report regarding the chain of custody of the computer tapes from one month prior to their disappearance up to the time they were loaded on the Zipp Courier van.

Who touched them? Who hired Zipp? When?

Who saw the boxes leave Global Financial?

Who drove the transport van? Which direction?

"I want to know everything about those computer tapes down to the second they left this building, and if safety protocols weren't followed, I want names. And, mark my words . . . ."

George paused without finishing the sentence. He would let each one fill in the blanks for themselves.

Maxwell thanked everyone for attending, not that they had any choice. He excused himself from the meeting and quickly walked to his corner office suite. George Maxwell knew he had at least two phone calls to make before the end of the day and before things got any worse.

He instructed his secretary as he passed her desk, "Helen, get me Oliver and Peter on a conference call right away to schedule a meeting. Tell them it's urgent."

CHAPTER FIVE

George Maxwell's life could have been marked with self pity and regret, but he chose otherwise. He was born Evan Mitchell to an unwed fifteen year old mother in White Plains, New York. She was a young and naive girl who had been charmed and misled by an upperclassman who was tall and handsome, an athlete and part of the popular crowd at their high school. He promised he loved her, but he quickly changed his mind and broke off the relationship as soon as he learned she was pregnant.

He refused her parents' phone calls, and in less than two weeks, he was pursuing another young lady, who was also taken in by his alluring ways. After high school, he left for college, and the Mitchells never saw him again. Their daughter never forgot him. He was her first love, and he broke her heart.

Evan's mother had the support of her parents, even though she had disappointed them with her actions. She realized that she would never be able to provide for him properly and finish her own education, and it wasn't fair to her parents for them to assume the responsibility of rearing her child. It was a hard decision for all of them, but together they agreed to give up the baby for adoption.

So, she and her mother contacted an adoption agency that advertised in a Christian directory. It helped to ease the pain and guilt she felt knowing that her son was going to a good home with two parents. Evan was adopted by an older, childless couple from the Midwest who promised to love him and give him a future, and who changed his name to George Evan Maxwell.

His new parents told him of his birth mother and the details of the adoption when he was old enough to understand. They told him they would help him try to find his birth mother anytime he was interested, but as far as George was concerned, he was the son of Mr. and Mrs. George Allen Maxwell of Highland Park, Illinois, a suburb of Chicago.

Even as a child, George enjoyed challenging adults and authority. His grade school teachers weren't accustomed to debating with children, so George usually caught them off guard. More often than not, he irritated the fire out of them. He had heard, "Because I said so," more times that he could recall. He also realized, even if his teachers didn't, that curiosity was a good thing. George wasn't afraid of the usual things that frightened other children: storms, scary movies, dark shadows, strange noises—only failure. He hated to lose.

He had promised himself when he grew up that he'd listen to people, young and old, especially those who challenged him and made him think. George was a delight to his parents, and they taught him strong Christian values as they had promised his birth mother they'd do. As he grew older, he enjoyed discussing the different doctrines and teachings of all religions, and he searched to find the meaning of his own. He felt he'd either better be able to defend his beliefs or else be ready to change them if he realized they were wrong.

For as long as he could remember George loved numbers and money. As early as third grade, he had amazed his teachers with his strong aptitude for math. By the time he was in high school he was completely enthralled with the world of finance and commerce. His hard work in prep school paid off, and he attended the University of Illinois on a full academic scholarship. There he earned his B.S. in finance in three years and graduated with honors, second in his class.

He had dreamed of going to Harvard. He knew others did as well and that each year only ten percent of over ten thousand applicants were accepted. The odds didn't deter George. He was driven, and wouldn't allow himself to consider rejection. Four years later, George graduated from Harvard with a doctorate of jurisprudence degree and his MBA. He was heavily recruited and turned down dozens of attractive offers in the Midwest at very reputable companies and law firms. But, George wanted to get as close as he could to New York City, the financial capital of the world—to Wall Street. Before he left his parents' home in Highland Park for the last time, he promised he would remember his Christian faith and teachings when making decisions about his life and career and when choosing his friends.

His first job was working for a medium sized bank on the East Coast to learn the finance business from the inside out. He began as a commercial lender responsible for developing relationships with new commercial customers. The bank's recruiter quickly recognized George's congenial personality and quick wit and knew he would do well in attracting new clients. He had his own key to the building and came and went as he pleased. He worked at least sixty hours a week, and was the first one to work in the morning, and the last one to leave at night. The security guards were accustomed to his work habits. He knew all the cleaning crew by their first names.

George's professional life left little time for personal relationships. It was difficult even to meet anyone of interest much less develop a serious or long lasting friendship, especially with women. He had dated a few interesting ones, but they usually lost interest after weeks passed without even a phone call. None of them understood how driven he was or how committed he remained to his career. Maxwell really didn't mind being alone; in fact, he rather enjoyed it. It gave him an opportunity to read or to review financial strategies for his high maintenance clients. He had his own personal goals to meet, and there was no time for distractions.

It was clear to his superiors that George had excellent analytical and strategic skills. He was easily able to review complex financial information for his wealthy clients and make appropriate and accurate recommendations. His proven leadership abilities and expertise had positioned him for a quick promotion to a senior investment consultant who reported directly to one of the executive vice presidents. He had helped create strategies and plans that incorporated competitive banking trends at both the state and national level, and always with a vision for the future.

After seven years, George was ready for a bigger challenge. Manhattan was one of the banking capitals of the world, and he had jumped at an opening with Global Financial Bank on Wall Street, close to the New York Stock Exchange and all the action. He had joined Global as a Vice President and the

Chief Lending Officer. His years of education, long hours and hard work were now paying off. This was the opportunity he'd been waiting for since college. He would have taken a lower position just to get his foot in the door, but they didn't need to know that.

George Maxwell's primary goal from day one at Global Financial was to outperform his competition and become number one. Now as the youngest President, Chairman of the Board and, CEO in Global's history, he was the best and brightest financial mastermind to come along in a very long time. The bank had become a world leader in financial services, with assets of more than seven hundred billion and operations in more than forty countries. It provided unparalleled services in investment banking, asset and wealth management, and financial services for customers and businesses and private equity. Global Financial was the second largest depository in the world for American and global receipts.

Maxwell knew whoever was behind this heist had a big head start on them all. It didn't matter. He was a natural leader, and he was finally at the top. And, no one, especially some little street punk, was going to bring down Global Financial. Not on his watch.

CHAPTER SIX

Oliver Burke, President and CEO of International Bank of Commerce, and Peter Gillette, President and CEO of One World Bank, agreed to meet with Mr. Maxwell the following week. In business circles, they were known as the Trinity, partly because they headed the top three banks with corporate headquarters in New York City and partly because they were alumni of three of the top business schools in the nation: Harvard, Columbia, and Chicago.

Although Maxwell didn't go into specific details on the phone, The Big Three pretty much knew why he had requested this meeting and why on such short notice. The local, as well as the national news, had carried the story of the stolen computer tapes, and letters to the editors of all the major newspapers were already pouring in. The media loved a scandal.

People were alarmed that so much personal data might now be in the hands of thieves. They were equally alarmed that the information had been so easily obtained. The public wanted answers. Law enforcement had stepped up investigations of complaints, and security measures were in place to detect unauthorized transactions at all financial institutions in the city.

A catered lunch helped with the scheduling. Helen Walker, Maxwell's middle-aged secretary, was accustomed to planning short notice meetings and luncheons for her boss. She had been the executive assistant to George Maxwell for five years and ran the secretarial pool, who reported directly to her like a jail matron. She was thick skinned and knew from experience that Maxwell's abruptness wasn't a sign of rudeness—just efficiency. Everyone had just so many hours in a day, and every hour was packed with work that needed to be done yesterday.

The caterers arrived at 10:30 and quickly prepared the table: cloth linens, silver service, and fine china, all arranged to perfection. Lunch was to be served promptly at 11:30. They offered mixed greens with pine nuts and a freshly made raspberry vinaigrette, pan-seared yellowfin tuna over wild rice, fresh melon with a mint leaf garnish, and assorted sherbets. The meal was tasty and nourishing, but not too heavy. Everyone needed to be alert. Helen knew what Maxwell expected, and she never disappointed.

The two men arrived at Global Financial Headquarters within five minutes of each other. Their limos wheeled into the underground garage where their personal drivers would wait patiently until they were summoned to chauffeur their bosses back across town.

Prior to the attack of September 11th, many corporate offices had occupied several buildings on Wall Street closer to the World Trade Center. But after 9/11 many of the structures were toxic and dangerous and had to be completely gutted and rebuilt. The other two banking corporations had to relocate their headquarters temporarily in lower Manhattan or across the Hudson River in New Jersey. Global Financial's Headquarters was farther away from the site of the attack, closer to the East River. It escaped major structural damage, and the business remained up and running on Wall Street during the repairs to its exterior.

The men rode together in the gold plated and mahogany paneled elevator that ran non-stop to the seventy-fifth floor. The elevator door opened directly into the reception area of Maxwell's presidential office suite. Helen immediately greeted and escorted them into the conference room adjacent to George's enormous corner office. She helped them get comfortable and notified her boss through the intercom that they had arrived.

The conference room was spacious and well appointed. The east wall of windows faced Brooklyn and overlooked the South Street Piers on the East River. Facing south, in the distance was a spectacular view of the Statue of Liberty, Battery Park and Ellis Island. Maxwell chose not to have any of his office or the conference room walls covered with vanity diplomas or awards. He knew who and what he was.

Instead, the rooms were decorated with designer tapestries and original art. Lighting was installed to highlight all the right places. There was live greenery, not that artificial stuff. Maxwell believed it added warmth to the room and enhanced the air quality. There were built-in shelves filled with hundreds of volumes of leather bound books, among them the classics, quick study references, world histories of politics and religions. He had read them all at least once.

George Maxwell straightened his silk tie, and slipped on his suit coat. He had a hard fast policy on dress. It was acceptable to remove your suit coat in your private office—behind closed doors, but no shirt sleeves in the hallways, and certainly not in public areas. Although there wasn't an actual written dress code for employees, everyone at the executive level knew what was expected: navy, grey or black wool suits with white cotton dress shirts and conservative ties for men. Women were also expected to wear reserved and understated business attire and sensible shoes, none of those trendy fashions, and certainly not that business casual some other offices allowed on Fridays.

Maxwell's suits were all tailored; twenty-two hundred dollars a piece. He loved the feel of fine fabrics and clothes that hung comfortably from his well proportioned frame. George was six foot three, one hundred and ninety five pounds. He knew his size was an asset.

George Maxwell opened the side door of his private office into the adjoining conference room and greeted his guests. They all exchanged the usual and expected pleasantries as they took their seats for lunch: "How's the wife?" and "What are the children doing?" and "Found any new vacation spots?" and "Read any good books?" As a courtesy, the two visitors let Maxwell lead the direction of the conversation as they ate. They arranged their food on their plates or sipped their coffee when there was a lull.

Once the meal concluded and the servers cleared the table, Helen Walker came in for one last check of the room. A tray of water and coffee was on the table. Notebooks, pens and paper were at hand. She exited and closed the double doors behind her. Maxwell sat at the end of the table with his hands folded. He knew that he must remain as composed as possible and display no sign of fear or panic. It was time for him and these men to address the seriousness and urgency of the situation. He chose his words carefully.

"Gentlemen, thank you both for taking time out of your busy day and on such short notice. I'm sure you are aware of the recent unfortunate events here at Global Financial Bank regarding the customer data that is missing and presumed stolen. Each of us in this room can appreciate the severity of this situation, and we, as leaders of our financial institutions, must act decisively so that our customers and shareholders will feel a sense of security about their assets." George stopped and drew in a long breath.

Oliver Burke took advantage of the slight pause and spoke up first. "George, you can be assured that we agree. My bank is still investigating our loss from last month. We'll share any leads we get with either of you men. If we don't get on top of this and find out who is behind it, every bank, locally or internationally, will be an easy target." Burke paused just a moment and then continued.

"I can't even imagine the panic we might see if our customers think their identities can't be protected. We're all facing chaos and the potential for protracted litigation if the lawyers smell blood and start advertising and encouraging the victims to join in a class action lawsuit." He looked at Peter Gillette who nodded in agreement.

"Oliver's right," Peter said. "This has gone far enough. Surely, those thugs must know we're not going to stand still while they wipe us out and destroy our customers' good names."

Peter had remained quiet until he had heard from the other two. He liked to listen and gather his thoughts before speaking. Now that the other two had voiced their positions, he continued.

"We all recognize a potential disaster that needs to be addressed quickly. But, we must use caution. Our goal is to tighten security without creating an unfriendly atmosphere for our own customers. I, personally, believe the public is already weary of all of the intrusions on their privacy. We've seen this nation's airports practically turned into a police state. Getting checked through security is at least a two hour process now for most domestic flights. People don't want to be herded like cattle and their every move watched and recorded."

Peter Gillette could feel his own frustration as he spoke. He knew the nation's security was the main reason behind all of the recent intrusions on his privacy, but he, like so many others, didn't have to like it.

"We have these surveillance cameras on street corners all over the city. At last count there are at least four thousand in Manhattan alone. The New York Civil Liberties Union can't even find them all. Just the other day, I saw six on one drug store on Broadway. No one can go anywhere anymore without the CIA and FBI knowing about it. So, George, it's not so much should we do something, the question is how? How do we protect our customers' information without adding to the atmosphere of Big Brother?"

Maxwell knew it was time to propose some new measures. "Thank you, gentlemen, I was certain we would agree and be able to work together to find some answers. My staff has put together some preliminary reports that explain the history of a technology I have personally researched and believe can be used to change the future of banking. The findings are in the notebooks in front of you along with a listing of resources for your own additional research."

The men opened their notebooks and began flipping through them as Maxwell spoke.

"As you probably already know, this nation, as well as nations all over the world, have been promoting the implementation of a national identification card. At first the idea may seem impossible. We might ask ourselves, 'How can this ever be accomplished?' and 'Do we have the proper technology to do this?' I say, yes, we do, and yes, we can. Please, gentlemen, turn to Tab Number Two and let me explain."

CHAPTER SEVEN 

George Maxwell was an avid reader. His personal library and collection included many original documents and first editions. Reading relaxed him, but also kept him up to date with the best seller list. Many of his colleagues played golf or tennis to relax. George read. He loved travel documentaries, Robert Ludlum and Tom Clancy thrillers, world histories, David McCullough biographies, do-it-yourself manuals. George loved knowledge. Even though his spare time was limited, he also loved to tinker with electronics and the latest technological gadgets. Several years ago, George had come across a report about an older technology, RFID, dusted off for use in the 21st century. It fascinated him.

RFID—radio frequency identification—had its early roots in World War II. The Americans, British, Germans and Japanese all used radar to warn of incoming planes. The only problem was, that there wasn't a way to tell which planes belonged to the enemy.

The Germans realized that if their pilots rolled their planes as they approached base, the radio signal changed. Hence, the ground crew knew they were German and not Allied planes.

Sir Robert Alexander Watson-Watt, a British scientist working on a secret project, invented the identity friend or foe (IFF) system. A transmitter on the plane exchanged a signal with a radar station on the ground that identified the plane as friendly.

George gave the bankers the abbreviated version of the history lesson. They could finish the rest on their own time. He continued his presentation with a rundown of the more current applications.

"Similarly, RFID uses wireless radio signals to transmit information. An original signal is sent to a transponder which either reflects back or broadcasts another signal. It can transmit the identity of either a person or an object in the form of a unique serial number, and it requires no batteries or human intervention." George paused to catch his breath and to give the others a chance to ask questions. They both were all listening intently, so he continued.

"RFID tags—minuscule microchips no bigger than a grain of sand—can store data in a computer system in digital form."

"Hasn't the public at large been using RFID, or some form of automatic identification technology for decades?" Oliver interrupted.

"Yes, but only in a limited capacity because of the low volume of sales and the lack of national or international standards to regulate it," George answered. "But, that's all changing."

He told them that recently the use of RFID had started to catch on in numerous and more widespread ways: anti-theft and keyless entry devices in cars, automated payment of toll roads without stopping, keyless access to office buildings and inner areas, tags in bracelets to locate children in theme parks. Many major companies and retailers were using tags on their products to track their location, which proved useful for controlling inventory and reducing lost or stolen goods.

At the gas pump, Shell and Exxon Mobil's Speed pass systems allowed loyal customers to use a wand, also called a fob or transponder, small enough for a key chain, to wave to a reader built into the gas pump. This allowed customers to quickly purchase gas without a credit card. Other major businesses, such as McDonald's, Taco Bell and KFC, were testing similar cashless payment systems for their customers, so they could pay for their purchases with a key fob.

Another example they all could appreciate was that Brinks security company had created a system in France to destroy money that was in transit in an armored truck if it strayed too far from an RFID reader in the truck. Further, the vehicles were equipped with a radio controlled homing device which could locate the truck and transmit its coordinates automatically and notify the appropriate law enforcement officials.

George Maxwell continued his monologue and tried to relay enough background information without boring or overwhelming the other two men. He wanted to convey how versatile this technology was with a lot of room for even more advanced uses. He knew they probably were at least somewhat familiar with the RFID tags and their use. He wanted them to know he was as well.

"So, George what does all of this have to do with us and the predicament in which we find ourselves? Cut to the chase. What do you have in mind?" Oliver asked.

"I agree," said Peter. "I'm sure you summoned us here today for something more than a science and history lesson, even though this is fascinating."

"Correct," said George. "I believe that with all the technology available through the use of RFID chips, we surely can come up with a more secure means for our customers to access their accounts, and for us to protect their personal information."

George revealed that his legal department was preparing an announcement and apology to go out to Global Financial's customers about the recent events. He guessed that it was similar to the letter they had sent to their own customers. He also shared with them his thoughts about looking to the future for a more secure method to protect his customers from anything like this ever happening again.

"I also have instructed my chief legal counsel, Elizabeth Hume, to research the possibility of implementing the use of more distinctive identifiers for our customers, such as fingerprints, iris scans, voice prints, and biometric identifiers. We need something better than our current bank cards. I believe this will enable us to tighten security measures and drastically eliminate identity theft and fraud."

"But, George, if an identification card is based on factors which can be forged or stolen in any way, how reliable is it?" asked Oliver. "How is it any better or safer than what we have already?"

"I'm wondering that, too," Peter joined in. "Let's face it, our world if full of thieves and there's little likelihood of controlling identity theft unless we take an entirely different approach."

Maxwell was pleased that his colleagues were attentive and open to debating the issue. "I agree, gentlemen," he said. "Even using the RFID technology, identification cards may not work, and they may not make us more secure. We all agree the issue isn't how well the card works when used by our honest customers. It doesn't matter how safe we try to make it if it still winds up being forged."

On page twelve of the notebook, something caught Peter Gillette's eye. It was a report about implanted computer chips using RFID technology in non-humans—to locate lost pets or stolen livestock, and to monitor the migration patterns of salmon in the Northwest. *Is it possible that this implanted "chip," this "transponder," could be used for human applications,* he wondered? He agreed, a bank ID card with a biometric chip full of unique identification data would be no safer in the hands of a thief than a PIN. *The criminal mind being what it is,* he thought, *we'll be right back here in no time trying to figure out how to address the theft.* But if the chip were embedded under a person's skin, it would all but eliminate the chance for valuable personal information or financial data to fall into the wrong hands.

Peter was lost in thought now, trying to imagine the full potential of this technology. *An injectable microchip—the size of a grain of sand, designed to work with a compatible RFID reading system. Is this where Maxwell was heading? It had to be. Maxwell was planning to promote the use of implanted chips in humans!*

"Peter, I see you've jumped ahead in your notebook a little. You're going to spoil my surprise."

Oliver glanced over to see where Peter was reading. "What surprise?" he asked and cocked his head toward George.

"Well, it seems that there is a human application for all of this technology. Flip over to page twelve." George summarized the report for Oliver, and Peter filled in with additional details he thought were noteworthy.

"Do we know how close this is to being marketed for human use?" Oliver asked with genuine interest.

George was cautious. He didn't want to relay false information and mislead his colleagues. "It's close, and the technology is available. We just have to learn how to make it work for us," he replied.

Peter was captivated by the idea, and wished he'd thought of it. His bank, One World Bank, had taken the largest hit of the three, and he needed to assure his customers that someone was doing something. Now that Maxwell had shared his vision with them all, Peter could take some of the credit so his own board of directors and shareholders would know that he wasn't sitting on his hands.

The three bankers continued to discuss their dilemma and other possible approaches, but most of their conversation came back to using the implanted computer chips. Each had reservations about any abrupt or drastic changes in banking. Many of their older customers were still a little leery of electronic transactions and direct payroll deposits. They believed there was just too much personal information floating somewhere in cyberspace.

Even in the day of cashless banking, people still wanted to touch and feel money in their hands. At least a bank card gave them something to hold. How would they react if that also was taken away and replaced with a computer chip or facial scan? But on the positive side, at least it would be difficult if not impossible to duplicate or steal a person's fingerprints or iris or voice prints, all verifiable identifiers.

The group agreed to keep their discussions private and to meet again when there was more to discuss and Elizabeth Hume's research was completed. There was no need to make any premature announcements that might upset the public anymore than it was already. They needed a clear plan of attack that would guarantee a solution. As usual, Maxwell was confident he could and would find one. Global Financial's legal department was unparalleled, and had protected Global from all sorts of calamities that had befallen other banks.

Global kept an array of trust and probate attorneys, tax attorneys and full time litigators on staff. They kept current on all aspects of the law and were gifted in keeping Global Financial Bank out of legal battles. George Maxwell looked forward to working with them, sorting through the all the legalities, and implementing a new state of the art in banking.

CHAPTER EIGHT

Elizabeth Hume had been a lawyer at Global Financial for fifteen years, long before Maxwell took over as CEO. But it was Maxwell who recognized her untapped talent and promoted her to chief counsel to the president and head of the legal department. This made her part of the senior management of the company. Elizabeth was a native New Yorker and proud of her Scottish heritage. Her grandfather, Samuel, left Leith, Scotland and arrived at Ellis Island on April 5, 1906, at the tender age of twenty-two. He signed in as Edward S. Home but later took on one of the optional spellings of the Clan name and in the new world became Samuel E. Hume. Elizabeth made a point to visit the museum at Ellis Island at least once a year. She went more often years ago when spare time wasn't such a luxury.

The museum was a living history lesson. She'd never forget the first time she'd walked through The Great Hall and researched *The Celtic,* the ship Samuel rode over on. She read the original manifest and found her grandfather's name among the passengers. There was a photo of *The Celtic*, built by Harlan and Wolff Limited, Belfast, Northern Ireland, 1901. It was twenty thousand, nine hundred four gross tons; seven hundred (bp) feet long; seventy-five feet wide; service speed 16 knots. It had room for 2,857 passengers (347 in first class, 160 in second class, 2350 in third class). Her guess was Samuel was one of the 2350. But they were all coming to America, regardless of class. From 1901 to 1903, *The Celtic* was the largest ship afloat. It was eventually stranded in Cobh Harbor, declared a total loss, and scrapped in 1928.

Elizabeth tried to imagine the trip from Scotland to America traveling in steerage—crowded and no doubt unsanitary conditions. What bravery these people possessed. They endured up to two weeks on a ship, sometimes on rough seas, headed for a strange land, uncertain of their destiny once they arrived. They had risked everything.

Elizabeth knew her way around the legal system and the political games in banking. She could face any jury or judge and could wisely and calmly advise Maxwell even in the midst of chaos. But she couldn't imagine what Samuel must've felt as he stepped off *The Celtic*, alone and scared, and made his way with a few cents in his pocket and all he owned on his back or in a small trunk.

She'd made a donation in memory of Samuel so his name could be placed on The Immigrant Wall of Honor. Recently, during one of her visits, Elizabeth pencil rubbed Samuel's name from The Wall onto a piece of paper. The etching sat in a small frame on her desk as a reminder to face challenges boldly.

She tried to remember her roots and Samuel Home, now Hume, anytime she needed to bolster her confidence. If he could succeed on strange soil and face the world with only his brain and two hands, how much more she should be able to do with all the resources she had available to her.

Elizabeth called a meeting of the most experienced and gifted attorneys from the legal department and their support staff the day after Maxwell met with his colleagues. She had her orders, and there was no time to waste.

"Beginning immediately," Elizabeth told the half dozen lawyers and paralegals in the room, "we will be working on a new project specifically requested by Mr. Maxwell. It is, of course, in addition to your regular assignments but will have top priority and is strictly confidential. It is not to be discussed outside these offices, not even among yourselves. All work is to be done in house. Store your notes and research in a locked desk at the end of each day. Plan to work overtime and weekends, if necessary, until it is finished."

As Elizabeth spoke, some of the lawyers exchanged glances. They were used to pressured assignments and confidentiality, but why all the secrecy? Elizabeth briefly paused to let it all sink in and then continued.

"As you know Global Financial, as well as other banks, is concerned about strengthening security for its customers. Mr. Maxwell wants to change the way customers access their accounts and he believes we can use modern technology to do so. We will need a comprehensive presentation to the board of directors so they can make an informed decision before approving such significant changes. I want to start with the history behind the push for a national identification card.

Larry, you and Christine will research the inception, as well as the current status of the program. We must include what other nations are doing with the use of a national ID and how well it's working."

She told them that the ultimate goal was for the bank to adopt the concept and rationale behind the national ID card for use in a new banking identification system that would enhance security.

"Andrea and Scott, I want you to assist me with the research on using biometrics as identifiers on a new bank card," Elizabeth said and the two quickly wrote down notes on the paper before them.

To the whole group Hume continued, "We'll also need to get an estimate of projected costs for such a system and a time frame to get it up and running. I'm looking for practical recommendations and applications. Our charge from Mr. Maxwell is very clear: to protect our customers' personal information, and to ensure confidence that we can guard their privacy. I don't need to tell you we'll be on the leading edge of banking reform. If successful, this will no doubt be accepted and duplicated by the entire banking industry, both nationally and internationally."

At times, the roomful of lawyers and staff nodded in unison as if everyone already knew all about their assignments. Their jobs were highly competitive, and each one strove to out-do the others for individual recognition. Occasionally, some of the paralegals wrinkled their brows as if to say, *What's going on?* But it was unheard for any of them to ever admit, although at times it was true, that they didn't understand something. It could mean their jobs.

Plans were made for another group meeting in two weeks to review the progress and to report on any problems.

As Elizabeth closed the meeting, she emphasized again, "Our first responsibility is to our customers. We must use whatever tools necessary to fulfill that responsibility. If any of you run into a snag, let me know immediately so I can redirect your search. Now, show me why you were selected and have the privilege to work at Global Financial."

Hume dismissed all of the team except Andrea and Scott. They had shown in the past that they knew the importance of discretion and could be trusted with sensitive information. They'd be working more closely with Elizabeth on the ultimate goal of the project, which was far beyond a new identification card. She gave them articles and books to read by morning on the history of RFID.

She confided that they were to focus more on the most advanced current use of biometric identifiers and the sub-dermal RFID microchip already on the market and used for security access. But, even though they were pledged to secrecy, she didn't and wouldn't tell them everything just yet.

CHAPTER NINE

The following week the letter of apology and explanation went out to more than one million of Global Financial's customers. The mailing list included anyone at risk, whose personal data was on the stolen computer tapes. That included customers with only a regular checking account that held just barely enough money to pay their monthly bills. It also included thousands of customers who had been loyal patrons of Global Financial for years, and the computer tapes contained information about all of their account histories, their personal identification numbers, lines of credit and numerous bank card transactions. If a thief had, in fact, gotten his hands on the tapes, which was very likely, it could result in a disastrous loss that could take a long time, if ever, to correct.

Elizabeth Hume personally drafted the letter and reviewed it with her boss until they were both satisfied with its contents and message. They wanted to include enough information to accurately convey what had happened and to warn the bank's customers, but they also wanted to assure them that Global Financial was on top of things. If problems arose as a result of the loss, the same quality standards that had driven Global Financial to such prominence still existed, and the bank would stand behind its customers until the last detail was completed to restore them and their losses. The message was to be clear: Global Financial accepted full responsibility and intended to make things right.

> Friday, July 1, 2005
> Dear Customer:
>
> The security of your account and personal information is of the utmost importance to Global Financial Bank. For that reason, we regret to inform you about the recent loss of computer tapes containing personal information about your accounts or loans with Global Financial Bank. This occurred on June 6, 2005, while these tapes were in transit with a third-party courier on the way to a secure storage facility.
>
> The tapes contain names, Social Security numbers, account numbers and payment histories of some of our customers. It is standard procedure for Global Financial Bank, as well as other banks, to provide this information each month to credit bureaus so that credit reports can be current and accurate. Global Financial Bank has always used bonded couriers with enhanced security procedures to transport this information. Nonetheless, several boxes of computer tapes were lost during a recent delivery.
>
> At this time, we have no reason to believe any of the information on the tapes has been used inappropriately.

However, we are making every effort to ensure that our customers are aware of this situation. We are offering any assistance you may need to monitor your credit and correct any problems, should they occur.

We recommend that you change your password and personal identification number (PIN). Do not use any part of your Social Security number as part of the new PIN or password. Also, Global Financial Bank has arranged for you to enroll in a credit monitoring service, at no cost to you, to help protect you from identity theft.

It is important to review your account regularly. If you discover any unauthorized activity, you must report it immediately to Global Financial Bank. If you believe identity theft or fraud has occurred, call our toll free hotline at 888-456-1111, open seven days a week, 24 hours a day.

Global Financial Bank is committed to the protection of our customer's confidential information. We regret any inconvenience or concern this situation may cause for you. We are taking appropriate and immediate measures to enhance our security procedures to provide the privacy and protection you expect and deserve.

Sincerely yours,
George Maxwell

Sarah Andrews drove from work at St. Vincent's Hospital and Medical Center in lower Manhattan and headed north to cross the George Washington Bridge. She merged onto I-95

North and headed to the New Rochelle Lincoln Avenue exit. Her apartment complex was on the south side of Huguenot Woods Park, and, if traffic was light, she could usually make it home from work in less than an hour. At times she took the subway and train and could catch a short nap. But, even though the parking garage fee was steep, Sarah preferred to drive into the city for work. It gave her a chance to think and unwind on her way home.

This evening she was exhausted after her second straight twelve-hour shift as the weekend attending doctor in the emergency room at St. Vincent's. She pulled into the apartment complex entrance, drove past the security post and stopped at the community postal center where she retrieved her mail that had accumulated over the weekend.

The road to her apartment building curved slightly to the left and continued past to a four-way stop where she turned right. Her unit was straight ahead. She parked her Saturn Ion in the assigned space in front of her door, gathered her purse, and headed into her safe place. As she closed the door of her apartment, she slung her mail, mostly bills and junk she assumed, across the kitchen counter and hurried to change into a tee shirt and sweats.

Lucy, her two year old Beagle, jumped and barked for her attention, always glad for the end of the day when her person got home. Sarah grabbed Lucy's leash off of the door handle which made her jump and wiggle even more. Lucy knew there were wonderful scents to explore on the other side of the front door and maybe even a treat or two after they got back from the adventure. Before they headed out, Sarah grabbed a bottle of water and, out of habit clicked on the television which was still set into CNN, the channel she had clicked off last night just before bed.

Sarah was a news junkie. She regularly flipped between Fox News and CNN for twenty-four hour coverage. Sarah could tell from the announcer's somber tone that the news at the top of the hour wasn't good. The trailer at the bottom of the screen confirmed it. She paused and headed for the couch in front of the television to listen to the report.

> Global Financial Bank, one of New York City's largest financial institutions with offices worldwide, has issued a statement and notice to its customers that confidential information was stolen on June 6, 2005, while in transit to a storage facility. The Bank confirms that there are no leads at the present, but it is doing everything possible at this time to discover the whereabouts of the missing data. Letters have been sent to more than a million individuals with detailed instructions on how to avoid identity theft if the personal information falls into the wrong hands. Global Financial Bank is asking its customers to review their records carefully and regularly for any suspicious activity on their accounts. There will be a special report tonight after the regular news about a new banking technology that uses embedded computer chips, programmed with biometric data designed to help prevent identity theft . . .

This wasn't good news. Sarah had opened an account with Global Financial Bank just six months ago when a new branch office had sprung up just a mile from her apartment complex in New Rochelle. She liked the Internet café, the personalized services, great variety of newspapers and the complimentary Starbucks coffee in the bank lobby. The atmosphere was inviting, with easy chairs and ottomans, and it looked more like a nice hotel lobby than a bank. Also, her fiancé, Scott Spencer, worked in the legal department at Global's headquarters in Manhattan, and he had urged her to make the switch.

She and Scott had met a little more than a year ago when Scott was out for an early Saturday morning jog through Central Park. There had been only a light dusting of snow the night before, but enough to leave a thin layer of undetected ice on his path. Scott's ankle twisted beneath him as he slipped and fell to the ground. He was hopeful that the ankle wasn't broken but grabbed a cab to St. Vincent's Hospital emergency room for an X-ray just in case.

Sarah had barely checked in for the day before Scott arrived. An orderly met him at the door to the emergency room and helped him into a waiting chair and wheeled him to an examination room. Sarah took a quick look at the swollen foot and ankle and ordered X-rays. Forty minutes later Sarah headed to the curtained room where Scott waited.

She had run track and cross country in high school and college, so the two of them compared tales about pulled muscles and torn ligaments as she reviewed the X-rays and examined his swollen ankle.

"It doesn't look like anything's broken, Mr. Spencer, but you'll have to keep ice on that ankle for the next twenty-four to forty-eight hours. And you'll probably need a mild pain reliever. An over the counter drug should be sufficient. Just take it as needed. Try not to put your full weight on that foot for the rest of the day and keep it elevated."

"Is that it?" Scott inquired as he began to dress. "Do I need to see a specialist or follow up with my regular doctor? I don't want to give up running, but I don't want to re-injure the ankle," he stated as he lifted himself off of the examination table.

"You can if the pain doesn't subside in a few days, but I'm pretty sure it'll be OK with the icing and pain relievers," Sarah answered with confidence and a smile. Scott liked both the smile and the confidence. Their conversation had been easy and natural. He hoped it would continue after she got off work

"Well, S. Andrews," he said as he squinted to read her name tag. "Would you be interested in making sure that I follow the doctor's orders? How about meeting for coffee or breakfast sometime soon? There's a great coffee shop a couple of blocks over that's not too crowded on Sundays around 8:30 AM."

Sarah had a hard fast rule: never date a patient. But, she had to admit this guy was different and so far, was fun to talk to. He was definitely flirting with her and she liked it. *So, what the heck. Some rules were meant to broken, weren't they?*

"You know what? That sounds like fun. I'd love to meet for coffee sometime. And the 'S' is for Sarah."

During the next year they seldom missed having breakfast together on the weekends, except for once a month when Sarah was on call in the emergency room. Scott lived in a townhouse in midtown Manhattan. He worked at least sixty hours a week and often took work home each day. Sarah commuted to work from New Rochelle. Both were usually too tired at the end of the day to be very social, so their schedules during the week made it difficult to see each other, which made the weekends special.

As the television announcer continued, Sarah jumped up, headed to the kitchen counter and grabbed her mail to sort through it. This one day, she truly hoped it was just junk and bills, and that she wasn't one of the unlucky million. Her heart sank as she saw the envelope with a Global Financial

Bank's return address. She ripped it open and slowly shook her head as she read the generic message, pretended to be from the President himself, Mr. George Maxwell. Yeah, he made it sound like he truly was sorry that his bank lost her personal information, and that he was concerned for her well-being. *Sure, you are,* she thought. *But how does that help me?*

Sarah felt a wave of anxiety start to stir. "Oh, please God, don't let anything bad happen to me because of this," she whispered and put the letter back on the counter. She pulled her long hair into a ponytail and out of her face before opening the door for Lucy.

"Well, let's get you outside for your walk, so I can call Mom and tell her to start praying." Lucy wagged her tail and wiggled all over in agreement as she headed through the door.

Melinda Andrews answered the phone on the third ring.

"Hey, Mom, how are you?" Sarah asked.

"Hey, baby girl." Even though Sarah was almost twenty-eight, she'd always be Melinda's baby girl. Melinda had waited longer than most of her friends to marry and have children. She was in her early thirties when Jacob was born, and two years later she had his sister Sarah.

"Well, I'm fine, but you don't sound so hot," Melinda said.

"Have you heard the news about the computer tapes lost by Global Financial Bank? It's been on the television."

"Yes, but I've not paid much attention to it. Why?"

Sarah explained the situation and how she'd received a letter from the bank president, and that she was one of the customers at risk. She and her mother talked about the possible repercussions, mostly bad ones, that could come of this and that Sarah should try to get hold of someone from the bank as soon as possible.

"Yeah, the letter gave a toll free number to call for help," Sarah added.

"Then you should use it and get as much information as you can."

"Mom, this is really upsetting to me. What happens if someone steals my identity? They'll run up charges against my credit that I may not even know about. Or, what if someone pretends like they're me and goes on some crime spree? I could lose my medical license while trying to clear my name. My career could be ruined. I've heard that stuff like that has happened to people."

By now Sarah was nervously twisting a strand of her hair as she spoke. It was a habit she'd picked up in grade school and was always a clear sign that she was nervous. Melinda could hear the anxiety in Sarah's voice. And, although she wouldn't tell Sarah, she could see how this could turn into a mess.

Instead she said, "Sarah, calm down. Nothing's happened so far. Let's just pray that nothing will. You may be getting worked up over nothing. Did the letter say what the bank is going to do to prevent this from happening again?"

"Well, the letter didn't go into any details, but I heard on the television report something about using an embedded computer chip. There's supposed to be more about it later tonight after the news."

Melinda's ears perked up. Did she really hear what she thought she'd just heard?

"What network and time is that going to be on?" she asked Sarah.

"It is either Fox News or CNN, at 9:00 P.M. Why?" Sarah replied.

"I want to be sure to watch it and hear it for myself," Melinda answered.

"Why?" Sarah asked, suddenly curious.

"Well, we just need to be very careful with all of this."

"Why?" Sarah asked, this time with even more persistence. "You sound concerned."

"Just be careful, Sarah. Don't do anything before talking to me or your dad. You don't need to let anyone put anything under your skin just so you can have a bank account," Melinda responded.

"I don't think it's any big deal. The implant is supposed to be pretty small, about the size of a grain of rice. I thought it sounded pretty cool, and I sure wouldn't have to worry about it being stolen," Sarah said, genuinely unconcerned.

"Sarah, promise me that you won't do anything like that," Melinda insisted. "I'm serious. This could be something very bad. We need to be careful and make sure we're not taking any marks we shouldn't be taking."

"Mom, you're not going to start that Bible stuff again, are you? I'm sure this is nothing. Now, you sound upset. I'm sorry I mentioned it. Let's just watch the program tonight, and we'll talk later. In the meantime, I promise I won't let anyone stick me with anything, OK?"

"OK, and stop pulling your hair," Melinda teased, but she wasn't smiling. She instinctively knew by now that Sarah was probably twisting a strand of hair to lessen her anxiety.

She placed the phone back on the receiver and picked up the remote to click on the television to try to find more information about the broadcast time for the story that evening. As she did, she could feel her own anxiety starting to build. All she could think of was, *Oh, dear God, this is it. It's starting. We must be ready. We must tell others.*

CHAPTER TEN

Richard and Melinda Andrews believed the Bible was the inspired word of God. It wasn't hard for Melinda to accept that. As a child, she'd been raised in the Southern Baptist Convention and was in church at least three times a week. Besides all of the services there were to attend, her father was a deacon, and her mother taught a Sunday school class and helped with the shut-ins and mission projects.

So, Melinda had heard about the lessons of the Bible even on days when the family wasn't sitting in the pews. She was baptized at the age of nine on the closing night of summer church camp. She was the fastest in her class on the Bible drills and had earned an award for perfect attendance every year before she left home for college. Even so, her teenage years were marked many times with loneliness and regret. She knew there was more to being a Christian than perfect attendance and memorizing Bible verses.

Once she left home for college, Melinda's church attendance drastically decreased, and her focus took a different direction. She decided she'd gone to church enough already for an entire lifetime and could slack off for a while. Besides, there were other things to learn and experience.

Richard had been reared in a very strict and formal Episcopal Church, where the priest conducted almost all of the services, and the parishioners simply knelt, sat or stood on cue when instructed to do so from the book of rituals. He, too, left home for college and quickly forgot all about the homilies he'd heard as a young man and altar boy.

Melinda and Richard met in a study group for a physics class their senior year at New York University. They were immediately attracted to each other and dated the remainder of the year. After graduation, Richard accepted a position with Colgate-Palmolive in Manhattan. Melinda was hired as a high school English teacher in New Rochelle, where they were married and bought their first home. They liked living close to the city, yet in a suburb with nice neighborhoods where their children could play safely.

The Andrews attended several churches in the community after they were married and when the children were still young, but they never could agree on one to join. It sometimes bothered Melinda that she hadn't instilled the importance of regular church attendance in her own children the way her parents had done for her as a child. She hoped and prayed that they would one day realize it on their own.

A few years after both of the children left home, and the house was quieter, the Andrews realized that their lives were unfulfilled and incomplete. Melinda had retired from teaching and had plenty of time to reflect on her childhood and the solid foundation her Christian parents had provided to her. She missed the closeness she'd once felt with other Christians. So, she and Richard agreed to visit a local church that was expanding and building a new facility closer to their neighborhood.

At the first service, they knew they'd found where they belonged. At the age of fifty, Richard was finally baptized after years of drifting from church to church searching for something that made sense of his life. Now they were members of a non-denomination Christian church and rarely missed a service. They loved to discuss with their friends from church at their weekly home Bible study meeting how Scriptures applied to daily living.

Each month the group picked a new topic to review, and everyone was encouraged to speak up and contribute. There were only eight couples in the group, which allowed for lots of lively discussion and friendly debate. About seven months earlier, the group agreed to start a study of the book of Revelation, mostly because they weren't quite sure what it meant, and they wanted to know more about future events. They sorted through several study guides and manuals and finally agreed to use a six week course titled *A Beginner's Guide to Understanding The Book Of Revelation, Level One.* Richard and Melinda set aside at least one hour at the end each work day to read the materials and answer the questions in the workbook.

At the end of the six weeks, the group agreed to continue to the next level of the program for a more advanced study of Revelation. *Level Two* was longer and more comprehensive and included cross references to verses in the books of Zachariah, Matthew and other apocalyptical sections of the Bible. It was then that the Andrews began to pay closer attention to the news around the world and possible fulfillment of the prophesies in these books. The weekly meetings became livelier. Discussion didn't need to be encouraged. Everyone was ready to speak up and contribute. The study guide made the mysteries of prophesy easier to unravel and understand for the most part.

But, even though they all read and studied and discussed and searched for the answers, they couldn't quite grasp the verses in Revelation that referred to the mark of the Beast. According to the Scriptures, the mark was the number of the Beast—or name or number of a man—and no one would be able to buy or sell without the mark or number of the man. And the mark would be in the right hand or forehead of all who took it. What in the world did all of this mean? No one knew for sure.

So, they all kept reading and studying and discussing and searching. It was fun and interesting to try to imagine what John and the other authors saw and heard as they recorded the visions of the end of the era. In the book of Revelation, John's descriptions were limited to the knowledge and technology of his day. He knew nothing about tanks and armored vehicles or nuclear rockets and bombs. The group had concluded that the visions described in Zachariah 14:12, wherein the people's flesh, eyes and tongues were consumed, most likely described the victims of a nuclear attack. They were also pretty sure there were hard times ahead for the entire world with unprecedented natural disasters, famine and destruction.

But, Revelation 13:16–18 foretold of a future event about the mark of the Beast that religious scholars and movie directors had tried to explain for years without much success. *Who was The Beast? And, what was the mark and the number of his name? Six hundred threescore and six. What did this mean? And why wouldn't anyone be able to buy or sell without it? What about Christians?*

No one knew the answers, but surely people wouldn't seriously print the number 666 on their right hand or in the middle of their forehead. That would be just too obvious. It had to be something more subtle than a glaring triple six in plain sight. The group agreed to take a break during the summer. Most of them took vacations or enjoyed yard and garden work. It would be a good time to step back from the subject for a while and think about what they'd learned so far. They'd come back in the fall and start fresh.

For the past year on the weekends Sarah worked her twelve hour shifts, her dog, Lucy, stayed with Melinda. The Andrews lived across town from Sarah in an older neighborhood on Riley Avenue. Lucy had met almost all of the neighbors and their pets, and she tolerated most of them, except for the Bailey's cat, Bubba, a few doors down.

At least once a day, Melinda took Lucy on a walk down Riley Avenue so Lucy could sniff for any new scents or intruders into the neighborhood. During one of their walks, Lucy spotted a squirrel and suddenly broke away from Melinda's grasp. She chased the squirrel into the Bailey's yard where she encountered Bubba who wasn't too happy to see her. Lucy quickly forgot about the squirrel and charged the cat. Bubba got in one swing of its razor-tipped paw before heading up the nearest tree. The gash across Lucy's nose looked serious enough for a visit to the vet.

"Oh, your nose will heal, Lucy, but I'm not so sure about your pride," Dr. Johnson said as he examined the cut. "These Beagles get on a trail or scent, and they're gone before you know it, Mrs. Andrews. You might tell your daughter about a new device that's now available. It's a tiny, rice sized chip that's injected just under the skin and stores information that will help locate lost pets. This new chip will eventually replace tags on all dogs and cats. It would certainly help find Lucy if she ever got lost."

Dr. Johnson cleaned the wound and applied a salve as he told Melinda all about the features of the injected chip and how it was supposed to be a foolproof identification that not only could quickly locate lost pets but also store their health history.

"How does it work? Is it painful to inject?" Melinda asked.

"Not at all. The implanted chip is also called as a transponder. It's a passive radio-frequency reading system. The chip is preprogrammed with a unique identification code that can't be altered. A low frequency radio signal activates it and transmits the code to the reading system and locates the pet."

Melinda wasn't quite sure she really understood everything the doctor was saying, so she just listened politely and nodded.

"Technology sure is amazing, isn't it?" she added.

"Yeah, and that's not all. I've also read that the micro sized bio-chip is ready to be put on the market for use in humans," Dr. Johnson added.

"Really? How would that work?"

"Oh, it's really not that complicated." Dr. Johnson explained that the implanted microchip would contain a person's

Social Security number, fingerprints, address, physical description, health, financial or military records, really anything about a person necessary for conducting day-to-day transactions.

"Say it's implanted in a person's hand, all he'd have to do is wave it in front of a reader to check out at a grocery or department store or to do just about any type of business. The possibilities are endless."

And then it clicked. Melinda couldn't believe her ears. She actually felt herself shiver as the vet's words registered in her head. *The mark! Could it actually be an implanted microchip, an electric transmitter, a transponder, whatever else he had called them?* Melinda tried to remember everything Dr. Johnson had just explained to her. She paid the bill almost absent-mindedly. Her thoughts were still on Dr. Johnson's last statement and how this new technology might supply some answers about the meaning of the mark of the Beast.

She gathered up Lucy, thanked the doctor and left. In the car on the drive home, Melinda hardly noticed the traffic around her. She stared straight ahead except for an occasional glance at her right hand on the steering wheel or her forehead in the rear view mirror. She drove down Meridian Street and stopped at the BP gasoline station on the corner for a fill up. She watched the dollar amount click off and wondered how would it feel to wave her hand in front of the pump to pay for the gasoline. She tried to recall the verses in Revelation . . . *That no man might buy or sell, save he that had the mark, or the name of the Beast, or the number of his name.*

Melinda looked all around the parking lot and watched the other people pumping gas or coming and going from the attached convenience store. Would these people understand and listen to the warnings and recognize the mark before it was too late? The new technology would appear to provide a tamper-proof security and hands-free convenience for all types of personal transactions, and with an implanted chip, the chance of personal and financial information falling into the wrong hands would all but be eliminated. It would appear to be the perfect solution to data control in every aspect of a person's life.

Melinda left the station and continued home. When she reached her neighborhood, she turned left onto Riley Avenue and drove past the nice homes with the beautiful mature trees that lined the street. Most of her neighbors had professionally landscaped yards and gardens. There were sidewalks on both sides of the street where her neighbors walked in the evenings. It was a quiet and friendly place to live. All of the neighbors looked out for one another. It looked and felt safe.

Tony Wallace was watering his front flowers and waved as she passed. He and his wife lived down the block from the Andrews, and their children had played together when they were young. As Melinda drove toward her home, she thought of her friends and neighbors in a new way. How could she warn them without seeming like a fanatic? How many would be sucked into taking the biometric implanted chip for the sake of convenience or security?

She had to tell Richard, then they had to tell their church friends. But, would their friends think that they'd lost their minds, and would they understand? It was so obvious to Melinda, but could she convince the others?

First, she'd better get together as much information as she could on this implantable chip before trying to convince anyone of its potential meaning and use. The more she knew, the better she'd be able to explain it to others, including Richard.

Maybe there was something in the *Level Two* program that she'd overlooked. It all seemed so overwhelming to try to piece together, she wondered where she should even start?

CHAPTER ELEVEN 

Before Sarah's phone call about the letter she'd received from Global Financial Bank, Melinda had put her research on the mark of the Beast on hold. She wasn't certain how to proceed and had convinced herself that she'd probably overreacted to Dr. Johnson's statements about the microchip. After the phone conversation with Sarah, and the second mention of an embedded chip for humans, Melinda knew she'd better get back to the Bible and the study materials on the topic. Sometimes it really took more than one nudge from the Lord to get her attention. He certainly had her attention now.

For several weeks she'd read every reference manual and study guide she could find on the subject. She'd spent hours researching on the Internet and at the major chain and Christian bookstores in New Rochelle. There were numerous articles and books, but all of the information eventually concluded the same thing—no one really knew for sure the exact meaning of the numerous verses in Revelation that referred to the mark of the Beast. But Melinda would not give up and accept that. *Why would God give us these clues if He didn't want us to know what they meant?* she pondered

Melinda and Richard studied the materials together and cross referenced all of them with the Bible verses to try to understand more. They were amazed at how much they'd learned so far, but it wasn't enough. They had to be prepared as much as possible when they presented this to their friends, and they had to be ready to discuss it with as much information as possible.

"Richard, let's look at out Bible concordance and see what the original text said," Melinda suggested.

He looked at her a moment. "Maybe that will help tie all of this together."

"All right," Richard agreed, "that sounds like a good idea."

The Strong's Exhaustive Concordance of the Bible was often used by teachers and students to locate any Bible Scripture or word and trace it back to the original Hebrew/Aramaic language that was used in the Old Testament and the Greek language that was used in the New Testament for a more precise interpretation. The Andrews kept a copy of the *Concordance* with their other reference books and had used it many times in the past to enhance their study.

Richard and Melinda sat at their kitchen table with fresh cups of coffee and placed their Bibles, *Strong's Concordance,* notepads and markers in front of them. Melinda wrote down all of the Scriptures in Revelation that mentioned the mark of the Beast so they could begin their search. The word "mark," as used in the verses in Revelation beginning with Chapter 13:16 and throughout the following chapters, was assigned the reference number, 5480. Richard quickly turned to the number in the Greek dictionary at the back of the book and began to read.

"Anything?" Melinda asked.

"Maybe. Look at this," he answered. Richard turned the large volume so they both could see it. Melinda's reading glasses hung from around her neck. She quickly pulled them to her face and focused on the entry.

> ***Charagma,*** *khar-ag-mah;*
> *a scratch or etching, i.e. stamp*
> *(as a badge of servitude)*
> *Charagma,* "to engrave" denotes
> "a mark or stamp," e.g. Rev. 13–16,17;
> 14:9,11; 15:2; 16:2; 19:20; 20:4

The Greek words were unfamiliar. Melinda slowly read them again and tried to sound out the pronunciation guide. She shifted her weight in her chair as she lowered her glasses and looked at Richard. "Could this mean something?" she asked. Richard slowly shook his head looking uncertain and hesitant to respond.

"It's hard to say," he finally offered, "but it sure sounds like it could be a clue to the meaning of the mark."

"I agree. It could be that this thing we presently call an injectable chip might have been what the Greeks would have referred to as a charagma, or a mark," Melinda said. "I'll make a copy of these pages and the chain reference guide .We can start collecting information and keep it in a folder as we run across it. We'll need more than this before we are actually ready to discuss this with our friends and see what they think. Why didn't we think to use this *Concordance* before?"

CHAPTER TWELVE 

Elizabeth Hume routinely reviewed the progress of the legal research and brief writing by her staff at their weekly departmental meetings. The final report was to be ready for the presentation to George Maxwell by mid-August. After that, a full report and presentation would go before the board of directors at its annual fall meeting in late October.

The board of directors was comprised of a majority of independent members as defined by the applicable laws and regulations and the listing standards of the New York Stock Exchange. As a general rule, a director was considered independent if the board had determined that he or she had no material relationship with the bank that would impair any independent judgment. There was a comprehensive list of factors that would help define a person's independence at the time he or she was proposed for election or re-election to the board. By maintaining this majority independence, the board of directors had provided strong leadership for Global

Financial in the past and had steered the company to the highest level of integrity.

Global Financial Bank's Code of Conduct expressed values that all employees, officers and directors were expected to follow and enforce at work and after hours in their private lives. In doing so, Global Financial Bank had managed to maintain a high standard of conduct that attracted high caliber board members. Maxwell knew that no matter how well the final report was written or presented, the new technology would never see the light of day without the support and confidence of the directors.

The weeks between the final presentation to Maxwell and the annual meeting gave him plenty of time to contact each board member individually and fully present all of the details of the proposal for the new security system. He knew they liked to receive plenty of advance notice of any major issues that might come before the board, especially those that might be controversial. Maxwell never called for a vote on anything that he didn't already know the tally in advance. He was good with the banking politics and knew how to get the support he needed from his board.

Elizabeth Hume had scheduled a rehearsal presentation to the entire group at its regular weekly meeting just prior to the actual presentation to President Maxwell. Each team had a separate report to distribute to the others so they could follow along during the presentation. Elizabeth had prepared questions in advance for the speakers so they could determine if they were ready to defend their research and positions just in case there was any opposition.

Larry and Christine spoke first. Part of their report detailed the status of all nations that were either considering or were actually using a national identification card. To their surprise, a national ID card was already in place in countries around the world, including most of Europe, South America, as well as the Asian countries of Malaysia, Singapore and Thailand. In Great Britain, the national ID card was still voluntary, but those who chose not to have one would at some point in the near future be unable to open a bank account, claim any government benefits, start a job, board an airplane, or buy gasoline. There was strong public support for a mandatory ID card, so it was just a matter of time. In many of the Asian countries the citizens were required to carry their ID card at all times, subject to prosecution if caught without it.

Although the United States had resisted and had outright rejected the idea of a national ID card for years, the United States Congress passed and President George W. Bush signed into law the Real ID Act of 2005 which mandated a standardized, electronically readable driver's license for all states to be in place by 2008. Even so, there was still plenty of debate and opposition to the idea.

"Supporters claim it will enhance national security, eliminate fraud and forgery, and guard against illegal immigration," Larry informed the group. "Opponents argue that the standardized driver's license will become a de facto national identification card."

"Why is that?" Hume asked.

"Because, it's supposed to be voluntary," he answered, "but a state driver's license will have to meet federal standards established by the Department of Homeland Security. And by 2008, anyone who lives or works in the United States will need this federally approved ID card in order to travel on an airplane, open a bank account, collect Social Security payments, or receive any other government benefits. So, the Real ID easily could become a national ID." As he spoke, some of the others in the room turned to the copy of the Real ID Act in the materials and read the report for themselves.

"Will there be significant changes to the new license?" Elizabeth asked.

"No, it won't appear to be that much different from the ones we already use, and individuals will still get the new ID through their state motor vehicle agency," Larry replied. "There still would be the basic information about the person: a digital photograph, date of birth, weight, height, sex, hair and eye color, and address. However, The Act proposes to use these biometric identifiers in an embedded microchip, called a smart chip, that would link all of the cards' users to a national data base," Larry stated.

Christine explained that actually the United States was trailing the rest of the world in the use of the smart chip and not just for an official identification card, but for all types of transactions.

"In Hong Kong, the Netherlands, and numerous European countries, ID cards embedded with RFID chips are being used for electronic cash transactions to pay for mass transit rides, meals at drive-through windows, recreational activities such as movies and ski resorts, as well as numerous other places where payment is usually made with cash," she stated.

"How does the chip work?" Elizabeth asked.

Christine gave a detailed explanation of how it was either active or passive and was used to identify a person or object by using a tag and tag reader.

"Passive tags have no internal power supply. Instead, a minuscule electrical current activated by an incoming radio frequency signal provides just enough power for the tag to respond. Active RFID tags have an internal power supply, such as a micro-sized battery, which enables them to store more information and last longer."

Christine went on to explain that passive tags were cheaper to manufacture with an estimated cost of about forty cents each to install in a bank card. With the expected increase in commercial use, it was predicted that the cost would significantly decrease to about five cents per unit. And, because there was no contact between the card and the reader, there was less wear and tear, and, therefore, was less need to replace it. It would be cheaper in the long run, and the bank would recover some of the initial cost of implementing the new system.

Larry broke in and explained that if Global Financial Bank chose to implement the new system, each customer would receive a new bank card containing a passive RFID tag with a smart chip that was programmed with the user's unique personal data. The data would be entered into a centralized base. The bank card would be scanned by readers in the corporate headquarters, branch offices, ATMs, and any bank that was equipped with the technology.

Typically, the reader provided the identification of the user and the time and location of the transaction. If the information stored in the central data base didn't match with the person trying to conduct the transaction, it would fail. A surveillance camera would tape the entire event, and any discrepancies would signal foul play.

Larry and Christine estimated that a system using a bank card with an RFID chip could be put in place at Global Financial Bank and its affiliates in less than a year. After additional discussions and questions, they concluded their presentation and took their seats.

Andrea and Scott took their places at the front of the group and began with an explanation of their research and the potential use of additional verifiable identifiers to be included in the new identification cards.

"Imagine using a unique physical description, such as your iris or fingerprint, to identify and verify that you are who you claim to be," Andrea began. "Each person would act as his or her own password, and a PIN would no longer be necessary to access your bank account." She hesitated a moment to give the group time to process the idea and then continued.

"Now, imagine not having to carry yet one more piece of identification, but to have all of this information permanently embedded so that all you had to do was just wave your hand in front of a reader to access your bank account."

Elizabeth knew where Andrea was headed and took this opportunity to break in and challenge the legalities of the concept.

"I'm aware that this technology is being used in animals, but, has it actually been approved for use in humans?" she asked.

"Yes," Andrea quickly responded and referred the group to a news release that was included with the materials that had been distributed earlier. She told them that in Mexico the attorney general and at least one hundred-sixty employees in his office had already been implanted with a device that allowed them access to secure areas of a new federal anti-crime information center.

Also, Andrea had read about a night club in Barcelona, Spain, The Baja Beach Club, that was using an embedded chip as a loyalty card. The chipped patrons bypassed the entry line at the door, and once inside kept track of their bar bill with just a wave of their hand. It had been in place since March 2004.

"But, what about use here in the United States? Has that also been approved?" Hume pressed.

"Yes," Andrea responded. "In late 2004, the Food and Drug Administration approved a device called the VeriChip for use in the medical field to confirm the identity, blood type and medical history of a patient. This chip is supposed to eliminate errors in medical treatments and save lives. This is similar to the chip used in the night club in Spain."

Scott took over the presentation and explained that the VeriChip was developed by Applied Digital Solutions in Palm Beach, Florida. Each chip contained a special identification number and customer information such as their Social Security number or other personal data that would insure their correct identity. The VeriChip was inserted just under the skin during a relatively painless procedure, but a local anesthetic could be used, if necessary. It remained dormant until activated by a RFID scanner.

A few in the room looked uneasy and adjusted in their seats as Scott described the chipping procedure. He quickly tried to address their noticeable discomfort by adding, "The process lasts only a few minutes and is much like getting a shot, certainly no worse that getting a tattoo, and people don't seem to be opposed to doing that. Presently, the standard location to insert the chip is in the triceps area, but it can be also placed in the underside of the wrist. The VeriChip is contained in a glass capsule not much bigger than a grain of rice. Once it's inserted, it is inconspicuous to the naked eye. It's designed to break or become unusable if removed, and it can't be lost, stolen or counterfeited," he explained with confidence.

Scott went on to inform the group that future uses include airport security, admission to military or government buildings, ATM access, and for credit and debit card transactions.

"It will eventually be a universal form of identification," he concluded.

"Wasn't a similar chip used to help identify bodies after Hurricane Katrina hit the Gulf Coast?" asked Elizabeth.

"Yes, morgue workers in Gulfport, Mississippi used the VeriChip to help keep track of the unclaimed bodies. The chips were implanted under the corpses' skin or inside the body bags for later tracking and identification," Andrea confirmed.

Scott and Andrea also found other information about an active RFID embedded microchip with a lithium battery that could be recharged by using a person's natural body heat.

"A government study had determined that a person's hand and forehead are the best sources of heat for optimal results," Scott reported.

That certainly made sense to Elizabeth, but any parent who'd ever checked a child for a fever would have known that.

"There's just one drawback to this type," Scott said cautiously. "The lithium battery has some unstable qualities and could possibly explode and cause a serious injury and soreness to the bone next to the implanted chip. So, I'm still researching for other options for an embedded chip that don't pose any danger to the user."

Elizabeth Hume was also familiar with another implantable device called the Digital Angel that Applied Digital Solutions had tried to market in 1999 and 2000. Its receiver was much larger and trackable by the Global Positioning Satellite, (GPS) and relayed information to a data base on the Internet where it was stored for future use. Applied Digital Solutions was unsuccessful in marketing the Digital Angel because of heavy opposition from the American Civil Liberties Union, libertarians, electronic freedom activists, and religious groups.

But that was all before the terrorist attack of September 11 and the increased need for security. Elizabeth knew that the public's mind set had changed, and now was a good time to promote a non-trackable version of the chip if the board of directors chose that direction for Global Financial.

Hume was pleased with the preliminary results of both teams' research and findings. She instructed them to continue to peruse the available information and update their reports as needed. Even though the FDA's approval for use of the VeriChip in humans was limited to health care applications, there was no reason to believe that approval for additional uses in security, financial, and personal identification applications wouldn't follow. It was persuasive that the practice was already in use in other nations. It could no longer be dismissed as a futuristic or science fiction fantasy.

Two reports would be distributed to Mr. Maxwell and Global Financial's board of directors, and they would bear the responsibility of choosing which technology to use. The first report would include the information Larry and Christine found regarding the use of an RFID chip in the conventional bank card form. The second report would cover the use of an embedded RFID chip that, when energized by a scanner, would provide the customers access to their accounts.

Elizabeth preferred the embedded bio-chip and saw it as a way to put Global Financial Bank on the international leading edge in banking. Another bank card with the bio-chip still would not be completely foolproof. There remained the chance that a thief could steal the card and assume the victim's identity. But, if the personal data were embedded under the skin, it would be safer and secure. The thief would have to remove the body part containing the device in order to use it. That would certainly call attention to an unauthorized transaction.

Thefts at the ATMs and retail stores would be greatly reduced, if not completely eliminated all together. Perhaps the banking and health care industries could unite and promote the sub-dermal chip as a way to manage and protect personal data for both purposes. The two industries had large and powerful lobbying groups at both the state and federal levels. If this idea was marketed correctly, it was quite probable that people would volunteer to get chipped as a way to relay medical information in emergency situations if they were unconscious or otherwise unable to communicate.

Yes, Margaret could see that this was a major solution to the identity theft problem that was becoming a nationwide epidemic. And, once again, Global Financial Bank would be a world-class leader.

CHAPTER THIRTEEN 

Vivo Solana had become a force with which to reckon. He owned, even though they were ill-gotten, the personal identities and profiles of more than two million people after the heists of The International Bank of Commerce, One World Bank, and Global Financial Bank. If a rancher or produce farmer in California needed thirty thousand fake identifications for illegal migrant workers, he could deliver. If a mafia head in Sicily wanted ten thousand bank account numbers to launder blood money, he could deliver. If a drug lord in Columbia needed fake drivers' licenses for dope dealers to rent cars and smuggle drugs across the border, Vivo was the person to call.

Solana was the king broker of personal information and stolen identifications. In the underworld, some were drug kings, others controlled prostitution or weapons sales. But Vivo controlled the market on supplying financial information and personal data.

Recently, Vivo had found another thriving demand for his product: desperate users of methamphetamine. Narcotics task force members reported the connection after repeatedly finding evidence of identity theft during meth lab raids. Vivo had first offered his commodity on the West Coast, home to thousands of meth labs. He was delighted when the demand for his product quickly spread to other parts of the country as the word got out.

In the last few yeas he'd made more money than he ever would have at an honest job with Global Financial Bank. He had excelled in the underworld and had become, through a well earned reputation, one of the leaders. He could buy and sell George Maxwell or anyone else at Global Financial Bank. He had bodyguards, stacks of money, nice toys—a dynasty. He was a king.

Still, Vivo didn't feel like a king. He'd mastered a life that was at odds with his grooming and training as a child. As cold as his blood now ran, he still hadn't learned to silence completely the voices of his now deceased parents that had encouraged him as a child to live an honest life. And, he couldn't turn off the memory of the one chance he'd once had to live that honest life that his parents encouraged, maybe not as rich as he was now, but certainly quite privileged.

But, most of the time the voice of revenge overshadowed those memories and his parents' voices. Despite the good voices, or maybe because of them, Vivo had learned to disconnect. The occasional, but necessary deaths were inconsequential, just business.

Solana would have preferred to prosper without the violence and in a way, that wouldn't require him to hide and operate under an assumed identity himself. He would have preferred to need his bodyguards because so many people loved and admired him as they did George Maxwell, not because the streets were full of traitors with demons of their own. Solana kept his guards close and in plain view. He wanted his "customers" to fear him, as they should. If he ever suspected they had broken their silence and exposed him he could arrange an accidental death or apparent suicide.

He was generous to those who were loyal to him and had learned that if he wanted to survive himself, he must eliminate those who weren't. Money and fear were great motivators to the people who did his bidding. He'd been loyal once but not adequately rewarded. He must not let those who discarded him continue to thrive.

He would have his revenge on the men who ruined his chance at financial success in the honest world, those who doomed him to be a king, but in the underworld. They had weakly and cowardly explained that it was just a business decision. He knew better, and now he couldn't let them get away with closing the door on him and forcing him to the dark side. They must suffer as he had. They must fall from grace and experience rejection, learn to kill to survive, as he had. So what if he took his revenge out on the personnel of Global Financial Bank? They deserved it.

Solana would show Global Financial Bank that it wasn't infallible. He had seen President George Maxwell on the news and read about his questioned leadership in the newspaper editorials and letters to the editors after the loss of the computer tapes. He'd seen Maxwell trying to reassure the customers and citizens that there was no need for panic and that their accounts were safe and insured. *Such arrogance, such pride, you've been untouchable for so long,* Vivo thought as he watched. *You want your customers to believe you're protecting their money and personal information. But, George, who's going to protect you and your board of directors and your shareholders?* Vivo sneered.

He had planned their destruction very carefully. There was no hurry. He'd learned patience while working hard, being loyal and waiting for his reward from Global Financial Bank. The records were safely locked away in a secure place until the time was right. So far, Vivo had only marketed the stolen data from the other two banks. He wanted Maxwell's customers to feel safe and believe that their information had not been compromised. He wanted Maxwell to believe that he'd been able to protect all of their precious money, and they had escaped any harm.

But now Solana was bored with the waiting. He needed some new action and to move forward with his plan to bring down Global Financial Bank. Enough time had passed and the public was feeling safe again and had relaxed its guard. Time to move and shake things up. In any event, Vivo wanted Global Financial to pay. He wanted to feel powerful against the legendary banking czar, George Maxwell. The time had now come for Global to face the calamity that the other two banks were suffering, to face the consequences of failing to recognize Solana's talents and expertise.

Vivo knew that if large amounts of money started disappearing from customers' accounts and they lost confidence again, they'd start withdrawing their funds and closing their accounts. If angered and disturbed enough, they'd refinance their personal mortgages and corporate loans with another lender; they'd cancel their bank charge cards with the lucrative interest rates and bank fees. They'd question the safety of their massive portfolios.

Perhaps if enough assets and net value started disappearing, shareholders would get nervous, perhaps Global's stock would fall. *It's about the money, George, not you, only the money.*

Vivo had even more surprises for the president and board of directors. He knew how to access *their* personal accounts, *their* passwords, *their* mother's maiden names, *their* Social Security numbers, *their* dates of birth. They all really had underestimated him. He smiled to himself when he calculated the value of Maxwell's personal profile and information along with that of the board of directors. The information would go for top dollar. Solana had even considered giving it away. He didn't need the money. The pleasure of watching the chaos was the only thing of value to him.

It was time to offer the stolen computer tapes from Global Financial to the hungry dogs of darkness. That would start the chain of events. Then, George and all of his colleagues would find themselves in the same compromised position as their customers. *It will be one king to another, George, just business.*

CHAPTER FOURTEEN 

Sarah knew something was wrong just as soon as she tried to withdraw $100.00 in cash from the automatic teller machine located in the hospital's lower level next to the employee's cafeteria. The message on the receipt indicated that her bank card had been refused and that her account was overdrawn by $1,730.00. That couldn't be.

Her paycheck from St. Vincent's Hospital was always electronically deposited into her account on the first day of each month. After her monthly payments for her rent, car and utilities were paid by electronic fund transfers, she always had at least a couple of thousand of dollars left for the rest of the month. And, she had overdraft protection for up to ten thousand dollars, and she knew for sure that she hadn't spent anywhere near that amount. Sarah was frugal with her money and diligently kept track of her withdrawals and transactions.

She tried the ATM again, thinking that there had to be some mistake. *No mistake.* The second receipt said the same thing. *One more time,* she thought. *Maybe I punched in my old PIN by mistake.* Sarah stuck the bank card into the slot and hit the code numbers again and waited. Still, there was no money and no receipt this time. She pushed the button to retrieve her bank card, but nothing happened. Again. Nothing. *What is the problem? Now I can't even get my bank card back to try at another ATM.*

She'd had her three attempts to type a correct PIN before the ATM confiscated her bank card. The employee credit union was closed for the weekend so no one was available to help, and she wouldn't be able to reach anyone with customer service at Global Financial until Monday morning. *Maybe Scott can help.*

Sarah pulled her cell phone from her pocket and slipped into the ladies' restroom around the corner to make the call. She was relieved that the restroom was empty. There was a sign placed very conspicuously at all of the entrances to St. Vincent's and next to the elevators on each floor that no cell phones were allowed to be used in the building. She certainly didn't want to be seen using hers.

Sarah quickly punched in Scott's speed dial number. After four rings, his outgoing message came on, so she pushed to end the call and turn off the phone. He'd been working on a really big assignment for several weeks getting ready for the board of directors' annual fall conference. *He's probably at his desk but has his phone turned off,* she thought. It wouldn't do any good to try to reach him through the main receptionist on a Saturday. All of the phones were switched over to an automated answering service for the weekend. This was her weekend to work the graveyard shift, so she wouldn't get off work until at least midnight, and he'd be in bed by then.

Sarah had just enough cash to eat in the hospital cafeteria that evening, but her car was almost on empty and she needed gasoline to get to work the next day. She had to get into her checking account soon. *If necessary, maybe I can borrow a small amount from Mom,* she thought, *just enough until I can talk to someone at Global first thing Monday morning.* In the few minutes she still had on her dinner break, Sarah called her mother. There was no answer.

"Well, this is just great," she said out loud and headed to the elevator and back to the ER.

Saturday evenings and early Sunday mornings were always busy. There were the usual victims of street crimes and domestic violence: the attempted suicides and drug overdoses, the sudden heart attacks and other life threatening situations. Weekends in the ER were never quiet. There certainly wasn't much time to sit around and think.

But even as Dr. Sarah Andrews worked to save a patient from death or collect evidence from a rape victim, she couldn't stop wondering why her bank transaction had been refused and her account was listed as overdrawn. There was an uneasy thought that kept at her. *What if someone else has accessed my account and drained it?*

She'd been diligent to change her PIN and to monitor her bank records just like the letter from Global Financial advised. Three months had passed and it appeared that no harm had been done due to the theft of the computer tapes with her personal data on them. Nothing unusual had happened, and she felt relieved and assured that her bank records were safe. She'd even managed to convince her mother that everything was resolved without any need for stronger security measures or embedded computer chips. At least the probing questions had stopped, and Melinda appeared to be relieved, also.

Now, Sarah wasn't so sure the danger had passed. She had never overdrawn her account. Something felt wrong. She hated not being able to talk to Scott or anyone to find out what was going on. Hopefully she'd be able to reach him in the morning before returning to work.

So far, Vivo Solana had been able to sell and distribute almost seventy thousand personal profiles and accounts from the stolen records from Global Financial. He'd patiently sorted through the data on the computer tapes and selected customers who had multiple accounts, a bank charge or debit card and a high credit line. These identities would bring top dollar on the market. Sarah Andrews was one of them.

He'd arranged for her personal data to be sold to another crook named Gloria Sanders in La Junta, Colorado, who quickly used it to drain Sarah's bank accounts, max out her charge card, and steal her identity to open new charge accounts and run up charges against them. The lucky buyer was pleased with Sarah's excellent credit history and high credit limit. She could easily hit this victim for close to a hundred thousand dollars before being detected.

Gloria was one of Vivo's loyal customers and had helped him in the past to distribute the stolen data from the first three banks to tens of thousands of the illegal immigrants who had crossed the border into New Mexico and Arizona. In return, Vivo made sure that Gloria got access to some of the better identities with higher bank balances and lines of credit.

Sarah Andrews wasn't the only Global customer who was having problems with her bank account. Thousands of others were discovering that they had overdrawn accounts also. Their funds had been drained, and checks were being returned to their creditors marked, "NSF." Additional bank fees were showing up on their monthly statements and on-line accounts.

By the time the merchant or creditor tacked on a fee for a dishonored or returned check and the bank charged its usual service fee for insufficient funds, customers were being billed for up to a hundred dollars extra, regardless of the amount of the initial payment.

The customers from International Bank of Commerce and One World Bank were having the same problems. Complaints were pouring in, and tensions were beginning to rise. Cashiers at all three banks were pulled off of their regular duties and assigned to the customer service stations set up in the lobby of each bank's corporate office and in several of the metropolitan branch offices. Extra phone lines were installed to answer questions from nervous or irate callers.

Even so, it was impossible to address all of the complaints from the desperate and disgruntled customers. The phone lines were jammed, and the long lines in the lobbies interfered with other banking business. The nightmare that all of the bank presidents had hoped to avoid was beginning, and there was no end in sight. It was time for action and to implement corrective measures that would help restore confidence and provide safety for future transactions.

Little did Maxwell know that Solana had already contacted his partner, Raul Vachon, in Geneva, Switzerland to set up the purchase of Maxwell's and the board of directors' personal account information. Vachon, like more than half of Geneva's citizens was an expatriate who enjoyed fame and fortune of questionable origins. He had many contacts in the seat of the European branch of the United Nations who had acquired personal wealth, but who had overriding privacy needs. Unfortunately, there were rumors of drug trafficking and graft often times associated with the wealth.

Solana and Vachon held each other in mutual regard, to the extent possible between thieves. Neither one trusted the other, of course, but they both recognized each other's talents . . . the only honor among thieves.

Vivo knew that Vachon would be able to traffic the sensitive personal data and make the most of its use. Raul Vachon had used International Bank of Commerce's Geneva's branch to launder multi-million dollar fortunes and hide money without any government scrutiny. He was familiar with the sensitive inner workings of banks and the shuffling of assets from one account to another if the appropriate personal data was available.

Oh, the personal wealth that was waiting to be transferred from Maxwell and his board of directors to the safe harbor of Geneva, a city of serial numbers.

CHAPTER FIFTEEN 

The last annual meeting of the full board of directors was on the third Thursday of October each year. All directors, without exception, were expected to attend this meeting held at the corporate headquarters in lower Manhattan. The committees and subcommittees were expected to have met well in advance of the fall meeting so that any information or materials important to the board's business could be distributed prior to the annual event.

One of the board's standing committees, the Public Responsibility Committee, was responsible for reviewing Global Financial's policies and practices aimed at maintaining public trust and confidence. Several weeks ago, in mid-August, George Maxwell received the final reports from Margaret Hume and sent copies to the chair of the Public Responsibility Committee, Doyle Jackson. Two days later, Maxwell called Jackson and requested a private meeting.

Jackson had been on the board of directors since 1999 and was generally supportive of Maxwell's vision and strategic long term plans to make Global Financial Bank the undisputed leader in international financial services. The two men had become friends as well as colleagues since Jackson's election to the board.

His background as president and CEO of a major communication corporation gave him valuable insight into successfully maneuvering government relations and was useful for developing corporate governance guidelines for Global Financial. George knew Doyle Jackson would help discover any weaknesses in the proposal for the use of the embedded computer chip when presented to the full board. It also would be beneficial if Jackson's committee helped to promote the concept and offer its full support at the annual meeting.

Jackson hadn't disappointed Maxwell. He was in full support of the idea, and he promised to call a meeting of his committee and submit a report to the full board within a month so it could be placed on the agenda in October.

George Maxwell awoke suddenly. He knew he'd been dreaming, but he couldn't recall the details. There was just a faint light starting to filter through the window blinds at 6:00 AM. Winter was definitely setting in, and the days were getting too short for his liking. He stayed in bed for a few minutes longer trying to recall his dream before concentrating on the day before him.

Sitting up slowly, George remembered that he was back in high school just days before graduation. He'd been lost in a hallway and couldn't find one of his classrooms for most of the semester. He needed the missed course to fulfill the requirements for a diploma, and he'd missed so many classes it was questionable as to whether he'd be able to graduate. In his dream, he wondered, *Is it possible that my college work and degrees could be stripped because I never graduated from high school? That's ridiculous.*

Maxwell got out of bed, relieved that it was just a dream. *Where do such absurd thoughts come from?* He wondered. George grabbed a thick Egyptian cotton bath sheet from the cabinet and stepped inside the polished black marble shower. The shower jets pounded his head and stimulated its circulation. Even though he could feel his senses stirring, the dream kept creeping back in, and he realized the theme had been a recurring one, just in a different form.

He recalled that not long ago, he'd dreamed for what seemed like all night long that he was traveling on a familiar road, but he never could find his destination. He was on a country road with several curves and side lanes and recognizable landmarks. But, just when he thought he had found the house he was looking for, the road would end abruptly or become impassable, and he could not reach his goal.

George shook off the night visions and directed his thoughts to the day ahead of him. The annual fall meeting of the board of directors was always a welcome event. It brought personal satisfaction to Maxwell to review the prior year and the bank's fiscal achievements. There had been steady and consistent growth in the assets and holdings every year since Maxwell had taken over as President. It was also good to see all of the directors in one room and try to ascertain if there were any dissidents among them. So far, George Maxwell had been so successful as Global Financial's leader, if anyone was opposed to him, he or she didn't dare let on.

Maxwell opened the double doors of his spacious closet with its custom-made shelves and drawers. He chose one of his best tailored charcoal gray suit and a new white shirt for the day. He let his fingers fan through the rich selection of hanging silk ties until they stopped at one with various shades of gray set off by black and burgundy accents. George slipped a silk handkerchief into his breast pocket and arranged its folds and creases until it met with his approval. He'd had his hair and nails groomed and shoes shined the day before. As usual, Maxwell felt quite comfortable and natural in the role he knew he was born to play.

He paused for one final glance in the mirror and studied the image before him. Yes, he looked the part. He was a man at the head of a world class financial operation, and he could and would lead it into the twenty-first century with a vision centered on being a global leader and catalyst for change.

His limousine was waiting at 7:30 AM sharp as Maxwell took the elevator from his penthouse suite and walked through the front door to the curb. "Good morning, Mr. Maxwell," the driver greeted as he held the rear door for George.

"Good morning, Reese," George replied as he slid into the warmed leather seat. "Let's stay on 5th Avenue for the entire trip downtown. I want to take in all of Manhattan this morning."

"Yes sir, Mr. Maxwell," the driver answered.

George Maxwell lived on the Upper East Side of Manhattan in a neighborhood that was named for the mansion that Andrew Carnegie built in 1901 at 91st Street and Fifth Avenue. Maxwell had moved to Carnegie Hill just after he was elected to the position of President and CEO of Global Financial.

The neighborhood was known for its gourmet food stores, upscale shopping and opulent homes. One could find exquisite glamour and fashion in which to indulge oneself. Maxwell frequently entertained business associates in the many superb restaurants in the area. He loved to enjoy the prosperity and comfort his life now afforded him. Carnegie Hill was a destination synonymous with the good life.

As they drove south on 5th Avenue toward the Financial District, Maxwell surveyed the passing hotels and gilded skyscrapers where fledgling businesses, opened by immigrants and pioneers chasing the American dream, once stood. He reflected on his own good fortune and the many milestones in his life. Even though he considered his birth and subsequent adoption an act of providence, George had to admit that there had been the occasional moments where curiosity led him to wonder what his life might have been like if he'd been reared by his young foolish birth mother.

Those thoughts were always quickly replaced by happy memories of his childhood and the realization of his good fortune of being adopted by a loving couple and reared in a privileged home. He'd received a wonderful education as a child and young adult and had been given exceptional employment opportunities and quick promotions. Already, his life had been extraordinary.

This day, too, would be another milestone for him. This day, Maxwell was optimistic that he would convince his board of directors to approve the use of the VeriChip for future banking transactions. He knew that his directors were coming to the annual meeting ready to hear some strong answers and solutions to the immediate problem of identity theft. The customers were getting uneasy about all of the fraudulent activity going on with their accounts. There had been rumors of possible class action lawsuits against Global Financial, claiming negligence in protecting the privacy of its patrons and in handling their personal data.

So far, the bank had been able to satisfy the victims by reimbursing any missing funds, removing all unauthorized charges and transaction fees and by offering to notify the three major credit bureaus of the theft and order copies of their credit reports. Global had also offered to provide complimentary fraud detector services for the next two years that would allow the customers to be notified within twenty-four hours if their accounts were used for cash advances, online, or international transactions.

Global Financial and the other two banks were doing everything they could to address their customers' needs and concerns. Even though there had been some hefty financial losses for some of their customers, the accounts were all insured and so far the losses had been covered. If all went as planned, Maxwell and Global Financial could escape from this potential scandal and emerge as a financial leader and innovator. As usual, Maxwell had tangible solutions to serious problems.

Ten days ago, the meeting agenda had been mailed to each director. They also received a brief synopsis of the expected presentation about the new technology so they could be somewhat familiar with the concept before the meeting. Maxwell had the only complete copy of both reports along with the statistics and supporting documentation. He had kept them in a safe at his townhouse for the past several weeks and had studied the reports at least twenty times as he rehearsed his presentation in his mind, imagining where he would pause and where he would stand in the room for maximum emphasis.

Of course, he would give due consideration in his presentation to a new and improved bank card with the RFID chip, but his goal today was to get board approval for the implementation of the VeriChip. It was the future of national and international banking, as well as a method to conduct unlimited global transactions. If Global Financial wanted to stay on top as a leader of innovative banking, it had to lead.

Just as soon as his board gave its approval to pursue the use of the VeriChip, Maxwell planned to call another meeting with the other two bankers. He knew there would be a great advantage to marketing this new technology to the public if the major players in the banking industry took a unified approach. Hopefully, the civil liberties advocates and religious groups would not protest as much this time around. And Global's customers would feel more comfortable with the new form of identification if other banks were doing the same.

There would always be the modern and cosmopolitan customers who wanted to be on the cutting edge of anything new. Maxwell knew that the new security system would especially appeal to them. It was the traditional and conservative average man or woman on the street who would be the most reluctant to accept the embedded chip. But, if the right marketing tools were used, even they could be won over.

After all, there was a time when a large portion of the population believed that the automobile was unnecessary and too dangerous. But Henry Ford had a vision that changed all of that, and the car industry expanded. George Maxwell had a vision also.

He envisioned a special day in the spring or early summer of next year. There would be a national news event during the early morning programs. All of the major and cable networks would carry it live. On the steps of Federal Hall, diagonally facing The New York Stock Exchange, George Maxwell and the other two bankers would stand together in the forefront. Several directors of each bank would stand on the steps behind their president, and right before the nation and the world, each president would roll up his sleeve and receive the painless sub-dermal chip.

They would then demonstrate its use and convenience with a portable scanner that could read the unique identification number in each chip. The hired spectators would clap and cheer and enthusiastically volunteer to get chipped also. There would be carefully planted recruits throughout the Financial District distributing flyers with information about the three charter banks, this new technology, and where a person could get in line to be chipped.

Back at Global Financial's corporate headquarters, the customers, new and old, would be treated to a catered reception with champagne punch, cake, and light hors d'oeuvres. Maxwell had set a goal of at least six hundred new accounts, opened before noon, using the new technology. A registered nurse would be present to inject the chip into all of the bank employees.

Maxwell wanted to insure that there was plenty of celebration and to send the message that the chip was safe and convenient. The word would spread quickly throughout the international banking community. The twenty-four hour news stations would carry the event over and over for the rest of the day. Those who missed the morning news would see it on the evening broadcast. The next day it would be on the front page of the business section of all of the major national and international newspapers. It would be a day in history for the entire banking industry. Global Financial would once again fulfill its nomenclature.

CHAPTER SIXTEEN 

The annual meeting began promptly at ten o'clock and was expected to conclude by early afternoon, absent any problems with the agenda. All twelve directors arrived within minutes of each other and made their way to the board room. They exchanged the preliminary courtesies to each other and took their seats around the massive table. They enjoyed seeing each other and appreciated the prestigious honor of being on the board of Global Financial. The trip to Manhattan was always worth the time away from their other responsibilities.

Two directors were CEOs of major oil companies. Some were leaders in the health care industry. One was a retired president and CEO of a college foundation for minorities. Two were heads of major media and broadcasting corporations. One was president of a large insurance company, and three served as corporate counsel to large businesses with franchises throughout the nation.

"Good morning, ladies and gentlemen, let's call this meeting to order," Maxwell said as he stood at the head of the conference table. After roll call the board got down to business and reviewed the minutes from the prior meeting. They were approved with little comment or discussion.

Next on the agenda was the annual financial statement. Maxwell was pleased to report there had been strong growth of the bank's net income over the prior year, mostly due to the growth in the core deposits and investment sales. Credit card revenues had increased by more than one billion dollars, and the banking fees and commissions were up due to an increase in sales of annuities and mutual funds. It had been a favorable year for Global Financial, and Maxwell had once again provided strong leadership.

Several directors posed questions regarding some of the line items, but after a few minutes, the annual report was approved, and the board unanimously agreed to declare dividends on the common stock. The board of directors quickly moved through the old business, after which fresh coffee and refreshments were served during a late morning break. Once everyone returned to his or her seat Maxwell politely silenced the group and directed everyone's attention to the next item on the agenda.

"We're now ready to discuss our new business. I hope you all have had the opportunity to thoroughly study the reports and information in the materials on the history of RFID and the VeriChip that were mailed to each of you a couple of weeks ago with this meeting's agenda. I know many of you have done your own research on this technology. I want to open up this portion of the meeting for everyone with any questions or comments to speak up so that we can thoroughly discuss and debate this issue. If we approve this new banking procedure, and I'm confident that we will, then we all must be ready to answer any questions that the media and public will have. And, we must be informed and confident with our answer."

Even as he spoke, Maxwell's mind remained focused on the presentation of the new technology that he was planning during the upcoming discussions. Elizabeth Hume and her legal department had been able to obtain a demonstrator VeriChip and scanner that would operate with a portable ATM. Doyle Jackson had agreed to help with the demonstration and play the part of the customer. They'd rehearsed a typical ATM transaction using the borrowed equipment several times, and each time the process went very smoothly and without any problems. Maxwell hoped that would be the case in the actual presentation before the board of directors.

"Mr. President, I have a question," one of the directors said after Maxwell finished the introduction of the new business item.

"Yes, the Chair recognizes Mr. David Cooper."

"How are we going to address and pacify the objections you know we're going to hear from the New York Civil Liberties Union and the ACLU? These privacy advocates will charge that the chip is the beginning of the end of civil liberties." David Cooper was Chairman and CEO of a world manufacturer of health care products. He was one of the most familiar of the directors with the VeriChip and knew the hurdles the health care industry had faced trying to get FDA approval for its use as a medical device.

Maxwell knew this question was coming and had already rehearsed his response. He realized if he did not present the answer in a confident manner, the directors would be left with doubts about Global Financial's ability to sell this to their customers. Maxwell slowly nodded, his expression serious, as he waited for Cooper to finish.

"Thank you, Mr. Cooper, for your question and comments. They show insight on your part." Maxwell responded to Mr. Cooper's inquiries by addressing everyone in the room.

"Mr. Cooper's concerns are very relevant and will need to be addressed. I believe his experience with this issue will help guide us through any objections from the protestors. I recall that these civil liberties groups had privacy safeguard concerns when the FDA was seeking approval of the VeriChip for medical applications in the United States. Mr. Cooper, with the board's approval, I'm asking you and our other directors with your background in health care to serve as a liaison with our legal department to help with any issues that already have been addressed during that process. There's no need to duplicate our research and responses. I believe we can assure these groups that banking security and civil liberties are not mutually exclusive."

There was unanimous approval from all of the board to Maxwell's proposal, and Mr. Cooper agreed to assist, as did the other directors who were heads of corporations in the health care industry.

Maxwell nodded to Hume, signaling her to step forward with Scott and Andrea to start the demonstration. "Ladies and gentlemen, we are fortunate to have the opportunity personally to observe the use of the VeriChip here today, a courtesy of its manufacturer, Applied Digital Solutions."

George was resolute in his belief that once people saw how simple the device was to use, they would realize its benefits far outweighed any fears they might have about privacy invasion. They would accept that it was a substantial way to prevent identity theft.

Preliminary discussions with the manufacturer of the VeriChip had assured Maxwell and Hume that their customers' privacy would not be compromised during use because the effective range for a scanner to read the embedded chip was only a few inches. Unless a user was positioned in close proximity to a reader, no personal information could be electronically intercepted and possibly misused.

"Ms. Hume, why don't you and your associates come forward for the demonstration now. Mr. Jackson has volunteered to get chipped, so to speak," Maxwell said, as he smiled and stepped back to make room for the presentation.

Wasting no time, Margaret applied the rice sized glass capsule with the VeriChip inside to Jackson's right hand with some adhesive tape. Scott and Andrea rolled the portable scanner within a foot of where he was standing and flipped a switch to activate the reader. Within a few seconds it was ready for use.

"Now, Doyle, wave your hand in front of the scanner so it can identify who you are," Maxwell instructed.

Earlier that morning, before the start of the meeting, Margaret Hume had programmed the chip's unique personal identifying number and Doyle Jackson's fingerprints, Social Security number and date of birth into the scanner. She had also entered close to fifty other randomly selected numbers so the scanner wasn't programmed just to read one entry.

Within seconds after Doyle Jackson waved his right hand, digital letters appeared asking what type of transaction Jackson wished to perform. He pushed a few buttons in response, and the room full of observers witnessed five crisp twenty dollar bills slide out of the portable ATM with a printed receipt.

Mr. Jackson successfully completed a few more transactions, all of which took less than a minute each. Most of the directors were on their feet by now, stretching their necks to maximize their view. Maxwell watched his colleagues as they observed the demonstration. He could tell they were impressed by the efficiency of the technology and process. Some of them smiled and nodded to one another after each transaction. Maxwell could hardly contain his pleasure.

Many great inventors had provided solutions to data protection with the use of encrypted messages and secret codes, and the use of passwords to access personal information had become commonplace. With the VeriChip, a numbered password or encrypted code would no longer be necessary. Each person's unique number, data and biometric features were his or her password.

"Very good, Doyle, thank you for being such a good sport," Maxwell said as he stepped back to his place at the head of the conference table. Margaret removed the chip from Doyle Jackson's right hand and disengaged the equipment before setting it to the side of the room, but still in plain view of the directors. Maxwell continued, "Let's all show our appreciation to our fine legal department for such a fascinating presentation." George began the applause, which spread around the room. "Now that you've seen this technology in action, let's talk about its future use at Global Financial," Maxwell invited.

He first explained that Internet banking would not be affected by the new technology. Global Financial Bank had already upgraded its Web-banking services by installing a login-analysis software that helped confirm a user's identity by asking a series of questions so personal only the legitimate user would know the answers. "The software will help to keep the costs of Internet banking at a minimum," Maxwell explained. "So, let's talk about the VeriChip." His tone became serious.

"For years I have been impressed with the caliber of the leaders of this banking corporation and your willingness to forge ahead with new and inventive methods of banking. Your courage and leadership has kept Global Financial in the forefront. I'm calling on you to step up once again and lead."

"Mr. Maxwell," a director at the end of the table, opposite from George, interrupted as he slightly waved and raised his hand for recognition.

"The Chair recognizes Randall Dixon." Dixon owned a large publishing company and newspaper in central Texas and had recently been appointed CEO of a national broadcasting conglomerate. Dixon was very familiar with First Amendment rights that protected an individual's privacy as well as the freedom of the press.

"I share some of the same concerns as Mr. Cooper, sir," Dixon began with a heavy southern draw. "This technology would certainly enhance a tamper proof identification and secure access for our customers. But, if we're fixing to install these readers and require our customers to take an embedded chip, aren't we just asking for protesters to picket outside all of our offices and the bank's headquarters for months?"

"How so, Mr. Dixon?" Maxwell asked.

"Well, I hate to even bring it up boys, but it seems to me that these civil liberties groups aren't going to be our only concern and opposition. I can just see where this embedded chip will give renewed ammunition to the religious zealots who will claim it is somehow related to the mark of the Beast. Global Financial doesn't need any more bad publicity and especially something associated with evil. How are we going to respond if these accusations arise?"

"I believe I can address that, if you don't mind," David Cooper offered.

"Certainly Mr. Cooper, anything you can advise on how to suppress or refute these allegations would be greatly appreciated." Maxwell said as others around the table nodded in agreement.

Cooper explained that to his knowledge the biblical reference to the mark of the Beast upon which the religious protestors relied, *required* individuals to receive a mark of some kind for all economic transactions. However, there was also a name and image associated with the mark and the number 666.

Clearly, if Global Financial allowed for the implanted chip to be voluntary, the chances of causing any alarm would be greatly reduced. And nowhere in the transaction was there any number that even remotely resembled the triple six. The VeriChip's memory could hold over one hundred characters . . . . . forty words . . . . . six lines, no 666.

Maxwell had also considered making the chip optional for Global Financial's customers as Cooper had suggested. "Thank you, Mr. Cooper. You've touched on a very valid point. We really haven't even addressed the option of using a new bank card with a RFID microchip that would operate much like the chip inserted under the skin. The front of the new card would have the customer's photo and Social Security number. A machine-readable magnetic strip on the card's back, much like that on a credit card, would contain a digital photo and the person's unique data. When the card was swiped through a reader, the information would be confirmed by the bank's database. Applied Digital provides both implantable and portable RFID identification. If we offer both options, then I don't see how the religious protestors could claim that people were being forced to take a mark in their skin in order to conduct financial transactions. People could *choose.*" Maxwell emphasized his last words as he concluded his point.

Randall Dixon appeared thoughtful as he looked around the room at the other directors and wondered if they were satisfied with Maxwell's response. After no one spoke, Dixon took the opportunity to call for action.

"Mr. Maxwell, I believe we have all had ample time and opportunity to consider these options. The demonstration of the chip was persuasive, and our discussions have provided satisfactory explanations to my own concerns. If no one else has anything to add, I'd like to make a motion."

The room remained quiet, so Dixon presented a motion which would allow both the new hand-held bank card and the embedded chip to be offered to Global Financial's customers. There was a quick second and the motion carried unanimously. The board of directors authorized George Maxwell to begin the process of ordering the equipment for Global Financial's corporate office and headquarters and all of its branch offices.

It was estimated that it would take several months before everything was in place, but the target date for the new system to be up and running was late spring, 2006. Official notices to the public would go out the first of the year. The board of directors concluded the rest of its business and adjourned right on schedule, just in time for a late lunch and socializing before the directors returned home on their evening flights.

In the late afternoon as dusk began to cover the city, Maxwell sat alone in the board room and reflected on the day's events. He'd instructed Helen to hold all of his calls and that he wasn't to be disturbed. George sat by the fireplace and opened the massive draperies covering the side windows so he could see the lights of the Bay. He felt conflicted but couldn't identify the reason at first. Why wasn't he more elated? He had skillfully manipulated the board of directors to completely authorize his agenda for the bank. He should be feeling like an esteemed ruler, a titan. But, he didn't. He felt tired and somewhat weary.

As George sat and thought about the discussions during the board meeting, he realized that he was bothered by Randall Dixon's comments. They stirred around in his mind and awakened an experience he'd had long ago. He recalled an event from his childhood when an old preacher had visited during a week long revival at the church he attended with his parents. George stopped to think and guessed he must have been about ten years old at the time.

Anyway, he remembered he was sitting with his parents on one of the front pews, close to the pulpit. He imagined that his eyes must have widened in disbelief as the preacher's voice got louder as he pounded his fist on the pulpit to emphasize his message.

The old prophet warned the congregation of a future event where people would have to take the number 666 in their right hand or forehead in order to buy or sell. The number was also called the mark of the Beast. The man's voice got louder and more urgent as he explained that the mark or number was from the Devil, and that God's people must refuse it, or they'd burn in hell for eternity. The preacher made a believer out of George, and during the altar call, he swore an oath to himself that he'd never ever put that number anywhere on his body.

Later that same night, George woke up from a vivid nightmare where he was being chased by someone trying to stick his right hand and force him to take the number 666. But, as George got older and the memory of that night faded, he dismissed all of that sermon as foolishness and scare tactics.

Now, more than thirty years later, George remembered that night and the preacher's warnings. Graham Dixon was probably right. Global Financial Bank would have to answer questions from the religious faithful about the embedded chip. They could argue that the chip appeared to be a type of a mark in the skin. *But, surely, this new technology couldn't be seriously associated with the legend of the mark of the Beast,* George thought. *The chip was to protect people, to promote safety, not result in eternal damnation.*

So, why am I even thinking about this? I thought I'd forgotten that old preacher and his nonsense a long time ago.

CHAPTER SEVENTEEN 

George Maxwell wasted no time in contacting the other bankers to inform them of the official action taken by Global Financial's board of directors. They all assured Maxwell and each other that they, too, would push for the same results from their respective boards.

Word spread quickly throughout Global Financial's headquarters of the future plans to install the new equipment. The accounting department began preparing the appropriate purchase orders for Maxwell and Elizabeth Hume to review and sign.

The legal department was once again busy reviewing all of the contracts and purchase agreements between Global Financial and Applied Digital, along with the waivers and releases that Applied Digital required of its customers. There was some concern about the informed consent language and the release of liability against the manufacturer that called for special scrutiny of the contracts.

Although the FDA had cleared the implanted RFID microchip, Hume wanted to make sure that Global Financial could assure its customers who chose to receive the VeriChip that it was safe and unlikely to pose any health concerns. In the event that anyone did experience an adverse reaction, Elizabeth Hume wanted to insure that Applied Digital stood behind its product and assumed all liability. The warranties were carefully worded, sometimes one-sided in favor of the manufacturer. It would take several readings to completely understand them all.

Scott Spencer spent hours reviewing and studying the warranties and contracts and writing memorandums to Hume about the areas he believed still needed to be clarified or further negotiated. The last thing that Global financial needed was for there to be undisclosed health risks associated with the VeriChip that later resulted in injury or a life threatening illness for its user. The FDA approval provided a large degree of protection, but look at what had happened to Merck with its drug Vioxx that had once been every arthritis sufferer's miracle pill. Global Financial was not willing to assume any of the risk, known or unknown, with the use of the VeriChip.

After the board meeting and the authorization for the new technology, Scott told Sarah about Global Financial's plans for the coming year and that a major fix was on the way to protect against identity theft. He let her know that he would once again be working long hours until all of the legalities of the deal were in place. He was grateful that she understood.

Sarah was glad that Global Financial Bank was taking an aggressive approach for a solution to the identity theft problem. She'd had to close out all of her charge card accounts and had spent hours trying to clean up her credit history because someone had assumed and stolen her identity and maxed out her credit lines. Thankfully, Global Financial had stood behind its promise to reimburse all unauthorized debits and charges against its customers whose personal data had been stolen.

Sarah had tried to say as little as possible to her parents about the ongoing problems with her bank account and charge cards. She was hopeful that everything would be resolved soon, and then she would share all of the details with them when she had more positive news. Sarah knew they would not be in favor of Global Financial's upcoming plans to start using the VeriChip, but she needed to let her parents know so the three of them could get their disagreements settled and behind them before next spring. Sarah waited until after the holidays were over before breaking the news. It was on one of the weekends that Sarah worked and took Lucy to stay with Melinda and Richard.

Sarah left her apartment early so she would have extra time to visit with her parents and explain the new technology before heading to Manhattan. The weather had turned cold and rainy, and the sky was completely overcast and gray, a typical January day in New York. Melinda met Sarah and Lucy at the door and quickly hurried them into the family room by the fireplace to warm up. She had a cup of hot chocolate waiting for Sarah and a treat for Lucy.

"Oh, burr, I just can't seem to get warm today," Sarah said as she huddled close to the fire and rubbed her hands together.

Melinda sat down on the sofa across from the fireplace and pulled her feet up under her.

"Well, I've not moved very far from my blanket and chair all day," Richard responded from his recliner. "It's a day to stay in, that's for sure. The weatherman is calling for light snow mixed with sleet later on this evening."

The three of them continued with their small talk and catching up on all of each other's news. It had been several weeks since they had been able to spend much time together. Sarah told them about some of the patients at the hospital and the tragedies that had come through the emergency room the last few days. Winter conditions and freezing temperatures always brought in victims of hypothermia, sometimes seeking treatment, but more often just looking for a safe place to rest and maybe something warm to eat. Sarah explained that the homeless migrated from shelter to shelter, including the area hospitals to stay warm and alive during the winter months.

As they spoke, Sarah was trying to figure out a way to divert the conversation to the real reason she had planned this visit. She found her opening when her father asked, "How is Scott doing? I haven't heard you mention him much lately, and we hardly saw him at all during the Christmas and New Year holidays."

Finally, Sarah thought. "Well, he has been working a lot of extra hours again lately, so we haven't seen that much of each other," she responded. "You know how our schedules conflict sometimes."

"Yes, you both have very busy careers. I don't see how you manage. Is he working on anything special?" Melinda inquired.

"Well, you remember all the problems that the bank had last June because of the theft of the computer tapes?" Melinda nodded in response to Sarah's question which prompted her to continue, "Apparently thousands of customers have discovered that their accounts were stripped and their identities stolen, just like mine."

"I thought that had all been resolved, and Global was taking care of all of the losses," Melinda said and quickly added, "By the way, how much did you end up losing?"

Sarah hesitated before answering, "I hate to even tell you, but maybe it will help you understand the need for something to be done so that nothing like this can ever happen again." Sarah told them about all of the trouble she'd had over the past several months, including her total loss in excess of one hundred thousand dollars.

She assured them that Global Financial had replaced all of the cash taken from her accounts and line of credit and had cancelled all fraudulent transactions at numerous ATMs located in the southwestern states and California. The thief had also used Sarah's personal data, such as her date of birth and Social Security number, to obtain new charge cards and had enjoyed a major shopping spree before those cards were confiscated and cancelled.

"Oh, my gosh, Sarah, we had no idea. Why didn't you say something?" her father asked as he sat up in his chair. As Richard and Sarah continued their discussion of the ordeal, Melinda listened and could feel a sense of apprehension creeping in. Sarah had lost so much, and there were thousands or maybe even millions by now in the same predicament. She realized that Global Financial Bank would be forced to take some very aggressive and corrective measures, or its customers would be outraged if identity theft occurred again and nothing had been done to help prevent it. Melinda waited for the right moment and then cautiously asked, "So, has Scott said anything about how the bank is going to safeguard its customers' information in the future?"

"Yes," Sarah answered.

"And?" Melinda pressed for more information.

Sarah reminded them of the television program from last summer about the RFID technology and the embedded computer chip. Melinda could feel the dread start to engulf her as her daughter spoke. She was certain where Sarah was headed with her response. Sarah briefly summarized some of the details and that Global Financial planned to issue an enhanced bank card at the very least. She hoped her parents would focus on the new bank card and less on the alternate method of banking.

"And, customers will also have the option of having the RFID chip implanted, but it's not mandatory," she stressed. "So, Mom, I hope you are not still concerned that this new banking process is *the mark of the Beast.*" Sarah lowered her voice and added a tone of apprehension as she emphasized the satanic reference.

"Sarah, I know that you think I'm overreacting, but your father and I did some more research on the verses about the mark of the Beast and traced them back to the original Greek language. The word, 'mark,' used in Revelation meant a scratch or etching in a person. It doesn't seem like too much of a stretch to me that something that is embedded in your skin could be the same thing that was described in the original Greek text."

"I share your mother's concerns," Richard quickly added. "You may be right in the end, and we could be way out in left field, but don't you think it's better to be safe than sorry on this?"

Sarah tried to address her parents' qualms by telling them about a medical product from the same manufacturer that was already in place at St. Vincent's and expected to be implemented at dozens of other health care facilities nationwide by the end of the year.

"The hospital has recently started using a system similar to the one the bank is considering, and it has been very helpful," she said. She told them how difficult it was to treat people who arrived at the emergency room when they were unconscious or impaired and couldn't relay their medical needs. If they already had the embedded device, a unique sixteen digit identifier in the chip could be activated by a handheld scanner, allowing immediate access to an electronic medical records system in less than a second.

"The stored information greatly reduces the delays in treatment and helps prevent medical errors. I just can't stress enough how valuable this new system is for our patients. It gives them a greater chance to receive rapid emergency treatment because we can determine immediately who they are, their medical history, blood type, known allergies and all sorts of vital information that could save their lives. The stored data also tells us who to notify in case of emergency and how to reach them. Patients' medical records can be automatically updated after every treatment, and only authorized hospital personnel can access them."

"You make a good argument, and I can tell that you have already made up your mind about this," Melinda said regrettably. "But, so have we. And I can't just stand by quietly and let this happen. When does the bank plan to start offering the embedded chip?"

"Not until late spring or early summer. Mom, what are you going to do?" Sarah asked with a sigh. "You know that Scott is working closely with the head of the legal department at Global on this project. Please don't do anything that's going to cause any problems for him."

"Well, I don't know for sure what I'm going to do, but I feel very strongly that this new technology will lead to privacy issues at the very least, and quite possibly . . ."

Melinda was interrupted when Richard asked, "Sarah, have you even considered the potential for harmful consequences of this new technology?"

"What do you mean?" Sarah challenged.

"What if we're right?" he asked rhetorically, his eyes pleading with her. "The problem is that we must think about what this device could be used for in the future. We may all agree that presently, its intended use is beneficial, but what happens if it is used for something beyond what is intended or it's no longer voluntary?"

Sarah looked skeptical but knew she could not sway them. Instead, she put on her coat and gloves and turned around to say goodbye and try to smooth things over. She bent down to kiss her dad goodbye and offered, "We just have a different opinion on this. Maybe we can talk more later and hopefully try to reach some middle ground. For right now, I guess we'll just have to agree to disagree."

Sarah crossed the room to where Melinda was waiting for her hug and kiss. "I've got to go, or I'll be late," she said respectfully as she put her arms around her mother. She reached down and patted Lucy's head and started toward the door.

Melinda walked over to close the door behind her. She watched as Sarah got into her car and drove away. "Lord, protect her, I pray," she whispered.

Melinda really didn't know for sure what she was going to do, but she had a good idea of where to start. Turning away from the door, she walked back to the family room. Richard had already settled into his chair again, but judging from the look on his face, he was still obviously troubled with what he had just heard from Sarah. Melinda stopped at the bookshelves where they kept their Bibles and reference materials and found the folder that contained their notes and research about the mark of the Beast from last year.

"Richard, I think it's time to talk to our friends about this and see what they think. We've put this off for months, even though we keep saying that we were going to bring this up at our Bible study group. This is at least the third time that I've felt the urge to dig deeper and try to learn what the prophesies mean and what will happen in the future. All of the other times, I got discouraged or sidetracked and just gave up and put it away. I always told myself that I'd get around to it, but once it was out of sight, I just ignored that little voice and convinced myself that I was too busy. But now . . ." Melinda hesitated as she prepared to commit to finally going forward with this plan. "We can't allow ourselves to procrastinate or be too busy any longer. This is just too important to ignore, and we'll need all the help and support we can get if we're going to oppose the bank and make an impact," Melinda said.

"I agree. Let's make copies of the information that we've found so far and bring it up at our meeting next week,"

Richard committed. "I've put it off, too, but it just keeps coming back. I don't think we can continue to keep quiet and do nothing."

CHAPTER EIGHTEEN 

In preparing for their next Thursday night Bible study, Melinda made a trip to the New Rochelle public library to copy all of her notes and the pages from the *Strong's Concordance* regarding the original Greek words that referred to the mark of the Beast. While there, she took advantage of one of the available computer terminals and got online to find Applied Digital Solution's web site. It listed several articles and news releases about the VeriChip and its use for security access control, asset tracking, and numerous health care applications for adults and children.

From there, she back clicked and typed in the word "VeriChip," which connected her to additional links for other access control systems that also used biometric technology to protect customers' accounts. To her surprise, there were many countries that were already using the VeriChip or a similar system. Apparently bank card crimes were not just occurring in the United States.

Melinda learned that in Japan, there were plans for a biometric based system in 2006 at several of the largest banking corporations. Japan's system identified customers at ATMs by scanning the palms of their right hand. The user's vein pattern was stored in an integrated circuit embedded in their bank card. Once properly identified, the customer was authorized to complete the transaction. It was anticipated that as more banks employed the new technology, convenience store ATMs which were linked to all of Japan's banks, would also adopt the system.

Melinda took out a pen and piece of paper and wrote down all of the different articles, then clicked on one that caught her eye about a pay by touch system in place at a mega-supermarket chain with stores located throughout Europe, the Middle East, and Africa where the customers' personal identification numbers and account number of their loyalty card were stored in a central data base. Then, after shopping, they accessed their account and paid for their items by scanning the index finger of their right hand at the checkout counter. This system was promoted by the manufacturer as the answer to all security concerns and the latest form of convenience shopping.

In Italy, the VeriChip had already earned a prestigious award for its role in improving the quality of life in the area of health care. Patients were utilizing the VeriChip to store and access their personal identification information and recent medical history. *This is exactly what Sarah was talking about,* Melinda thought.

It was apparent from the numerous articles that the technology was perceived to be the state of the art in medicine and security access around the world. But Melinda couldn't escape her fears that even though someone might originally agree to have a chip implanted in his or her hand as a medical identification tag, the same chip could also be used to replace credit or debit cards or even cash for business transactions.

Melinda returned to the related listings under the VeriChip search to see if there were any others that interested her. To her surprise, she had previously missed a selection about halfway down the page in the middle of all of the sponsored links and web results. There was a listing entitled, "Shopping with 666 and VeriPay." Her eyes widened as she clicked onto it. The site opened immediately. She stared in amazement as she read the introductory paragraph written in bold print. It was Revelation 13:15–18!

> "And he causeth all, both small and great, rich and poor,
> free and bond, to receive a mark in their right hand or in their
> forehead;
> And that no man might buy or sell except he that had the
> mark or the name of the Beast or the number of his name.
> Here is wisdom. Let him that has understanding count the
> number of the Beast, for it is the number of a man and his
> number is Six hundred, three score and six."

As she scrolled down the page, she could feel her thoughts spinning. Her eyes traveled across the words faster than her mind could process them. *Wait. Go back.* Something had caught her eye. It was an article released almost a year ago about a plan for all United States citizens eventually to take the VeriChip. President Bush's former Secretary of Health and Human Services, Tommy Thompson, was now on the board of directors with Applied Digital Solution! He was expected to help Applied Digital accelerate the adoption of the VeriChip for health care and security applications.

The article went on to explain that Thompson had the chip inserted in his arm back in September 2005 as a demonstration of confidence in the technology. He acknowledged that it ultimately could be used to conduct financial transactions, on a voluntary basis, of course. Melinda leaned toward the computer screen as she continued to read the article. She felt a sense of revelation as the words flew past.

This is exactly what Richard and I were talking about, Melinda thought. *This device will be marketed as the answer to all sorts of worldwide issues—emergency health care, security breaches, lost or stolen pets and children. The potential use and market for this technology is unlimited!* Melinda hit the print button. The cylinder clicked into place and began pulling the sheets of paper through the printer.

Melinda left the library with copies of several articles and web sites for even more information, if necessary, to share with their Bible study group. As she drove home, she tried to sort through the information in her head and wondered what it all meant. Melinda couldn't wait to show Richard all of the new research she had found and to get his reaction. She hoped their friends would be as convinced as they were about this technology and its potential for harm. Sure, it sounded good, but it quite possibly could be the precursor for something that ultimately would become very evil.

Melinda wasn't sure where all of this would lead, but she sensed that they were on a path of no return. The more she dug into this topic, the deeper she got. One article led to another. Each new word search opened hundreds of pages of yet even more information on the injected chip. It could take hours to fully discuss everything she had found. From what she had learned at the library, the use of the embedded chip was already in place on a global scale.

How did it make its way into the international markets without anyone hearing much about it? Why weren't more people as uncomfortable with this as she and Richard were? How would they ever be able to stop this? Many thoughts flew through her mind, but one in particular kept coming back. "Who is like unto the Beast? Who is able to make war with him?"

The Thursday night group met at the home of Dan and Jean Baker, who lived a few blocks over from the Andrews. They had a comfortable and spacious family room in the lower level that could accommodate a large number of people. There was an inviting stone fireplace on one side of the room with a family-sized eating bar in the kitchen area on the opposite end. A competition-size pool table backed up to the oversized wrap-around sectional sofa, and a fifty-four inch screen television allowed for clear viewing from any spot in the room.

The Baker family had five adult children, eleven grandchildren and more friends than they could ever count. They had never met a stranger and graciously offered the use of their home anytime their church had a need. So, when the study group first organized a couple of years ago, Jean Baker spoke up and quickly volunteered their home as the meeting place.

Melinda and Richard Andrews arrived early for the next scheduled meeting to help Dan and Jean arrange the seating area and to set out some light refreshments. Each couple took turns bringing appetizers or a dessert to share with the rest of the group. This was the Andrews' turn, and Melinda had prepared one of their favorites—her Aunt Bessie's recipe for carrot cake with a cream cheese frosting.

The first fifteen to twenty minutes of each meeting was always set aside for socializing and catching up with each other's news. The cake was a welcomed surprise, and no one worried about the calories as each sliced a generous portion and poured a cup of coffee.

As the group made its way toward the sofa and chairs with cake and coffee in hand, Dan explained that Melinda and Richard would be in charge of the presentation for the evening. After Dan opened the meeting with a prayer and an update of several prior prayer requests, he turned it over to the Andrews and sat back to enjoy his refreshments as he listened.

Melinda set the stage for her presentation by telling the others of her conversation with Dr. Johnson last summer about the embedded chip for animals and the chilling effect it had on her as he spoke. She then summarized all of the problems associated with the identity theft that Sarah had experienced due to the stolen computer tapes.

Several in the room nodded as they recalled the news reports of the theft. After Melinda finished, Richard spoke up and gave a brief explanation of RFID technology and the use of the implanted chip in humans. "Melinda, would you mind?" Melinda stood up and distributed copies to everyone of the background information, as well as the notes, they made from the entries in the *Strong's Concordance.*

"OK, now that everyone has a few of the details that started us on this quest, let's look at the verses in Revelation and the original Greek words about the mark of the Beast,"

Richard said. The group followed along as Richard explained the process that he and Melinda had used to trace the words used in Revelation to the original Greek language.

Terry Walton was the first to speak up. "So, what exactly are you saying? What do you think this means?" he asked. He was one of the more outspoken and skeptical members of the group and was always ready with lots of comments and questions.

"Well, we can't say for sure, but when you break down the phrase, 'the mark of the Beast,' and take just the word, 'mark,' in the original text the word meant a scratch or etching in the skin," Richard replied.

Terry was not so sure about that as evidenced by the frown that crossed his face. He used a different translation of the Bible—The New International Version. He read out loud the same verses from his Bible and pointed out to the others that it said that the Beast forced everyone, small and great, rich and poor, free and slave to receive a mark *on* his right hand or *on* his forehead, not *in* as Richard suggested. The group eagerly turned to Richard for his response.

"What do you make of that?" Dan inquired.

Richard smiled as he explained that he and Melinda had run into this same discrepancy with their own research and found that the *Strong's Concordance* as well as the King James Version of the Bible relied upon the *Original Textus Receptus,* the earliest manuscripts of the Scriptures from the fourth century. Other translations, such as the New International Version, used the *Stephanus Concordance,* which most Bible scholars believed was not as reliable. The *Original Textus Receptus* translated the Greek word, *epi,* the preposition in the phrase, as meaning a mark in the hand.

Terry did not respond. Instead, he reached for Richard's Bible to compare the two verses. The frown returned to his face. As Terry read silently, Richard found his place in his notes and continued with his presentation. He informed the group that it was likely that some of the major banks—Global Financial for sure—was planning within the next few months to introduce to the public an embedded chip.

"This chip, will contain all of the customer's personal information, and it is inserted just under the skin," he explained. "Could this incision be the same thing as a scratch or etching in the flesh where the chip is inserted? I don't know, probably not," he confessed. "Right now, the chip is being hailed as the state of the art in banking security. But, what happens when grocery and department stores and the cleaners and all of the drive thru services start using the embedded chip to transact business, and the chip becomes just a miniaturized debit card, and no one can buy or sell without one?"

The speculation stimulated a lively discussion and debate of all of the possibilities that could arise with the use of the chip. Melinda told them about her own search, which resulted in finding several articles about the mark of the Beast linked to the VeriChip. In the middle of the debate, Terry finally spoke up, his expression serious.

"This is amazing," he said pointing to the middle of a page in his Bible. "One little word can significantly change the meaning of the entire verse. Even so, I don't see how we can afford to take a chance with this and allow one small word to make any difference. Does it really matter if it is on the skin or in the skin? But, what are you suggesting that we do?" he asked Richard.

Richard glanced at his wife, who gave him a nod of encouragement. "Well, Melinda and I do not think there is any question but that we have to voice our opposition to this embedded computer chip." Richard hesitated then continued with his response. "But, I don't see how our little group here will make much of an impact. We'll need more people, and I'm hopeful that we can get other Christians to join us on this."

"To do what?" Jean asked.

"For starters, we could contact some of our other friends and other churches that might be interested and just as disturbed at the potential harm in all of this. We could also explore the possibility of setting up a telephone campaign and maybe even a protest rally in downtown Manhattan," Richard answered.

Terry again was pensive as he listened to the others' enthusiasm as they bounced around ideas. He finally interrupted to voice his concerns. "Before we get all stirred up about this, we need to make sure we're on the right track," he warned. "We've all heard about these fanatics, these fringe groups that come out against any modern technology and say it's the Devil or Devil worship. We don't want to come across as alarmists and lose all credibility."

Terry went on to remind the others of all of the people who got caught up in the Y2K panic right before the turn of the century. Millions of people worldwide, Christians included, had predicted that the world would turn upside down when the computers that controlled all aspects of daily life failed to recognize the year 2000 and shut down. Hucksters made a fortune selling freeze dried food and gas powered generators for electricity. Gun dealers bragged of record sales. People by the droves moved to isolated farms in the country or to remote cabins in the mountains to become self-sufficient and hide from the masses who failed to prepare and came looking for help.

"Remember how we heard about tens of thousands of people, *Christians included,"* he said again for emphasis, "who hoarded food and water and vowed to use their guns against one another if chaos broke out? The world sat and held its breath as the clock ticked over to the year 2000 across the multiple time zones. If we come out in opposition to the banks and the embedded computer chip, I just don't want us to let our protests get out of hand so that we end up looking like a bunch of kooks and no one listens to us," Terry concluded.

"I fully agree," Richard said when Terry was through making his point. "The stakes are high, and if we're careless, it will greatly jeopardize our credibility."

The others also nodded in agreement. "OK, so let's pledge that we'll keep each other informed about any actions we plan to take and that we'll jointly preview any letters to the editor prior to making them public," Terry suggested.

"I agree," Richard concurred with a nod.

Melinda looked around the room and watched as her friends embraced the idea. She was delighted with their enthusiasm and support. It was an answer to prayer, and she knew in her heart that they were on the right track and must take a stand against this embedded chip.

In the morning she would make an outline of all of the ways they could alert the public and sketch out a rough draft of a news flyer for distribution in grocery stores, laundromats and other public places. She made a note to herself to call about a park she remembered that was located in lower

Manhattan that would be a perfect place for the protest rally. Hopefully it could be scheduled close to same time that the bank planned to announce its use of the embedded chip. The group concluded their questions and discussion and agreed to review their plans at the next meeting.

On the drive home, Richard was more talkative than usual as he enthusiastically recounted the evening's events. Melinda tried to pay attention, but was distracted as her mind turned back to the conversation that had occurred a few days ago with Sarah and her plea, *Mom, please, don't do anything that will cause problems for Scott.*

It wasn't Melinda's intention to cause any harm to Scott or to anyone at Global Financial for that matter. Her purpose in bringing all of this to the public's attention was to alert them so that they could avoid the potential for future damnation.

As she reflected on the meeting, Melinda was aware of the mixed feelings that stirred inside her. She was torn between her convictions and sense of duty to God to oppose the chip and her desire to avoid conflict with Sarah and Scott. Even so, she knew what she must do. It could mean saving them from danger.

CHAPTER NINETEEN 

There were at least three churches in New Rochelle and two more in White Plains that held the firm and uncompromised belief that the Bible was and still is the true inspired word of God. Jean and Dan Bakers knew many members of each church, and they had agreed to contact their friends and invite them to join the protest. Time was short. Everyone was pushing to get the message out to the communities.

In just a matter of a few weeks, the Bakers were able to recruit enough people to form a solid base from each church, and word quickly spread. Everyone who was interested encouraged friends and family members to join, and quickly a human chain of information linked out to every town and suburb north of New York City, between the Hudson River and Long Island Sound all the way to the Connecticut border.

Jean and Melinda put notices of Global Financial's upcoming event and the protest rally in the local newspapers in both cities. They gladly paid the expense, and the ads ran twice a week in the days just leading up to the announcement date. They also posted information flyers on the community bulletin board at some of the larger grocery stores.

Letters to the editors of the area newspapers began pouring in. The majority of the writers were more concerned about the potential risk for adverse health results after injecting a RFID chip into a human being. What was the bank thinking? Had Global Financial thoroughly examined the potential liability if things went wrong for its customers? And just who was going to pay for all of this new equipment? In fact, only a few of the writers addressed or mocked the religious objections.

The metropolitan citizens had certainly seen their share of crazies, so they didn't get too worked up over another doomsday prediction. It wasn't exactly the reaction the Andrews had hoped for. They had preferred that more customers would openly object and threaten to leave the bank. But, on the positive side, at least people were talking and not blindly agreeing to the bank's plan without questions. So far, the plan was working. People were reading the ads and responding.

The letters to the newspapers and the editorials were not lost on Global Financial. It, like all banking corporations, had a public relations department that was responsible for perusing the daily newspapers of all of the local and major cities both nationally and internationally in order to compile good press releases for their shareholders and web site and to watch for negative reports as well. So, early on Global Financial caught wind of the controversial notices and planned demonstration that was scheduled to occur on the same day that the bank planned to announce the new banking procedures.

George Maxwell came across one such editorial in *The New York Times* as he drank his early morning coffee at his desk two weeks before the date of the planned announcement. At first glance, he was flattered and amused that the editorial staff would even devote *any* time or space to the story. As he got further into the piece, he stopped smiling as he reread the paragraph about the predicted opposition from the American Civil Liberties Union, the New York Civil Liberties Union and, "a religious fringe group calling the chip, 'the mark of the Beast.'"

Oh, no! he thought with exasperation. George had hoped to avoid any negative publicity. Originally he had naively envisioned that the chip would be broadly welcomed by the public and recognized as the technological advancement that would drastically reduce, maybe even eliminate identity theft. In spite of Randall Dixon's comments, Maxwell had never seriously considered that it would be even remotely associated with the mark of the Beast like the newspaper stated.

What is the matter with these people? They sound like that old preacher who scared me to death as a child. Why do they have to be such fanatics about everything? Maxwell read on about the protestors and their plans on the day of his company's transformation. They sounded determined about their beliefs and weren't likely to back down easily. *We'll see about that.*

George Maxwell was agitated. He didn't want a handful of protestors to be able to sway the public's opinion about his company and the future of banking. In fact, Maxwell had been on edge a lot lately, but he just thought it was due to the flurry of activities necessary to get ready for the change over to the new systems. There was so much to do, and it had to be perfect. But now he wasn't so sure that was the source of his agitation. He didn't need one more irritant. *This implanted chip is a great idea and the future of commerce. I am not going to allow* *<u>one</u>* *thing, and especially a bunch of Bible thumpers and civil liberty rabble rousers, to cause any problems.*

Maxwell reached for the button to his intercom. "Helen, get Elizabeth Hume on the phone for me and try to set up a meeting for later this morning, maybe over lunch. Tell her it won't take very long, but I must talk to her today."

"Certainly, Mr. Maxwell. I'll get back to you right away."

"OK, listen carefully," Elizabeth instructed Scott and Andrea. "I had a meeting with Mr. Maxwell yesterday afternoon. I haven't seen him this intense before about anything. And, he is very agitated about all of this negative press the bank has been getting over the new RFID bank card, and especially the implanted chip. I told him we can't stop anyone from publically protesting or speaking out against it, as long as they remained civil. I tried to explain that people do still have their Constitutional rights, even though they keep getting watered down in the name of national security. So, he wants to take another approach."

Elizabeth explained to the two that Maxwell firmly believed if he could just meet with some of the protestors and maybe answer their questions or address their concerns, then he could smooth things over. In other words, if he couldn't silence them, perhaps he could persuade them. That had always been one of Maxwell's strengths, the ability to convince his opposition that he was really trying to help, not hurt them.

If that didn't work, Maxwell had another play. He knew that he could make a few phone calls to some key people and make it more difficult for the protestors to get through the streets around Federal Hall. All he'd have to do was request extra security due to the perceived threats, and the surrounding blocks would be closed off to cars and pedestrians. That would really irritate the morning commuters and create a lot of negative feelings toward the protestors.

Maxwell didn't want to play that game, but he would if it meant getting the new technology out to the public on time and with the appropriate fanfare. He absolutely would not tolerate a situation where he had to yell over a protestor. And, as always, he would not accept failure.

From several of the sources of information it was apparent that the protest was initially organized from a grass roots effort that started in New Rochelle with a handful of believers. If George could just meet with some of them, perhaps he could convince them to tone it down a little.

Scott had hoped to avoid any conflict with Richard and Melinda over the bank's plans. He'd hoped to stay out of the middle of any debates. His hopes were suddenly fading.

"Well, I could probably help with that," Scott reluctantly spoke up. "I know a few of the individuals who are involved, and I could speak to them and try to set up a meeting."

"Oh, really? Who do you know?" Hume asked with surprise and curiosity.

"Actually, I know the original organizers. They're Richard and Melinda Andrews. They're the parents of the woman I've been dating, and I've heard all about their objections for several months now. I didn't say anything sooner because I was hoping they would back down and forget all about this. Instead, it seems as though they are more determined than ever to gather as much opposition to this as they can."

"Do you think they would meet with Mr. Maxwell?"

"I can't say for sure, but they're really nice, good people, and I can't imagine they would refuse or be mean spirited about this. I can ask, if you want. When would he want to get together?"

"The sooner the better. Mr. Maxwell really wants to quash the negative press. He'll probably try to meet with representatives of the New York CLU also. Why don't you talk to the Andrews right away and get back to me?"

"Of course," Scott responded with a forced smile and feigned enthusiasm. This was the very thing he didn't want to happen. Now, not only was he in the middle of the debate with Sarah and her parents, but also, he was now in the position of messenger boy between the Andrews and George Maxwell.

Scott hurried back to his office, his head spinning with questions. He wasn't a betting man, but he couldn't help but wonder what were the odds that he'd find himself in such a sensitive position? *Let's see,* he thought with a sense of doom, *who do I want to alienate the least: the parents of the woman I love, or the man who holds my career in his hands?*

CHAPTER TWENTY

It really wasn't as awkward as Scott Spencer thought it would be. In fact, Richard and Melinda Andrews were very agreeable to the idea of about personally meeting with George Maxwell to discuss the implanted chip and their concerns.

The actual public announcement and demonstration of the new technology was a little less than two weeks away. Maxwell had carefully timed the day to correspond with the one year anniversary of the theft of the computer tapes that occurred on June 6, 2005. So, Scott had only a few days to try to coordinate everyone's schedules. Maybe if he spoke to Sarah she'd be able to help smooth things over with her parents.

"Sarah, please tell your mother to back off. I'm caught in the middle here."

"Hey, you've met her. How much good do you think that will do? She and Dad are both involved, and I've said all that I can."

They agreed that it was probably better if Scott dealt directly with her parents, and she stayed out of it. The next day he dialed the number for Sarah's parents, hoping to catch either Melinda or Richard at home.

"Oh, Mrs. Andrews, I'm really glad I was able to reach you," he said after Melinda answered the phone on the second ring.

"Well, hello, Scott. What a surprise. Is everything all right? You sound a little anxious."

"Yes, I'm actually calling from my office, and I've been really busy all morning and probably have had way too much coffee. Sorry. I'll try to slow down a little. I hope I didn't sound too abrupt."

"Of course not. Sarah's told us that you've been working extra long days lately, trying to get ready for the bank's big announcement that's coming up."

"Yes, that's true and well . . . uh, that's actually the reason I'm calling." *Come on, Scott, stop stammering. You sound like an idiot.*

"Oh?"

"I have a very special favor to ask of you and Mr. Andrews."

"Well . . . I hope we can help. What is it?"

Scott briefly explained the reason for his call with just enough information to try to interest them in a meeting with Mr. Maxwell. He would let his boss fill in the blanks when they were all together. He was relieved and audibly sighed when Melinda and Richard accepted the invitation.

They concluded their conversation after scheduling a lunch date for the following week. Scott agreed to accompany them to the meeting if that met with Mr. Maxwell's approval. He would get back to them the next day with the exact location and time of the lunch date.

"What do you suppose that's all about?" Richard asked after Melinda hung up from her call with Scott.

"Hmm, very interesting," Melinda said with an incredulous expression on her face. "That was more than just a courtesy call. Sounds like we may have got Mr. Maxwell's attention with our campaign, and he wants to talk about it. That's good," Melinda said as she slowly nodded her head. "I've got some things that I want to say to him myself."

CHAPTER TWENTY-ONE

St. Maggie's Café was a favorite spot for business luncheons and the corporate crowd from the Financial District. It was conveniently located at the corner of Wall and South Streets. Scott had set up a lunch date for the following week after the Andrews agreed to a meeting with Maxwell. The night before the appointment, Melinda and Richard met with their friends from church for prayer. They all knew that this meeting could be a big waste of everyone's time if Mr. Maxwell was not even a little open-minded about their objections to the use of the new embedded chip.

Melinda and Richard parked at a nearby garage by the South Street Seaport and arrived early at St. Maggie's. The weatherman had predicted a thunderstorm to hit around noon, and they didn't want to get caught in traffic. They waited in the lobby area near the bar and front dining room. There was also a rear dining room with several tables carefully arranged to accommodate the guests but spaced appropriately to allow for a semi-private conversation. Melinda and Richard had heard of this restaurant from some of their friends and had read the critics' reviews, but they had never had the pleasure of dining there.

Melinda looked around the room. She was struck by the beautiful and elaborate architectural details of the woodwork, especially near the stairs and balcony. There were several men and women, dressed in business attire, already seated and engaged in serious discussions while waiting for their food. The ambiance of the café and the buzz of the numerous conversations in the room hinted at the many deals that previously had been struck over a drink or power lunch within the confines of the small, but elegant Victorian setting.

Richard and Melinda quietly studied the diverse internationally-inspired menu on display as they waited for their host to arrive. It offered Chilean king crab croquette, curried chicken, sesame ginger salmon, and wild mushroom ravioli as some of St. Maggie's signature features. They all sounded good, and maybe under different circumstances, Richard would have been more tempted to indulge himself. Today, he didn't have much of an appetite. Melinda's stomach twitched as she recognized her own apprehension of the meeting before them. She quietly prayed for God's guidance and peace.

The front door opened, and Melinda turned to watch as Scott Spencer and George Maxwell entered. She watched as the maitre d' greeted them and collected Maxwell's overcoat and neck scarf. Due to the inclement weather, the temperature had dipped to the mid-sixties. Scott disliked the bother of a coat and opted for one of his heavier wool suits to protect him from the chill.

Melinda could hear Maxwell's rich bass voice that carried throughout the room. At first, Melinda was puzzled and thought she recognized it. *Had she actually met him previously and forgotten? The voice sounded so familiar.* If so, she couldn't remember when it would have been, but it was possible.

As Maxwell began walking toward the Andrews, Melinda watched him even closer. The glare from the front windows made it difficult for her to see his face clearly, but still, he looked vaguely familiar. *He probably has one of those faces that always reminds people of someone they know,* she thought. She could see that he was tall and fit with dark hair, but that could have described several diners in the room. There was something else. *What was it?*

While George Maxwell waited for Scott to introduce him and he greeted his waiting guests formally, Melinda finally got a full front look at him. He was very handsome. His eyes were familiar. The voice, the physique, the gait, the mannerisms—all familiar. Her heart began to pound. She could feel her mouth begin to water as her throat tightened, and she swallowed hard.

Although the features before her were not completely identical to a past acquaintance, they stirred memories of long ago, of things that Melinda believed she had forgotten. She imagined that she must have had a bewildered look on her face, but she couldn't control her reactions.

She looked directly into George's eyes, but looking back were the eyes of a young man she had known many years ago. She watched as Maxwell reached out to shake her hand and then Richard's, but she couldn't move. She felt paralyzed and drained of all energy. Memories flooded her brain, and her chest ached as her heart pounded inside her. For what seemed like several minutes, Melinda could not move or speak.

"Honey, are you all right? You look like you have seen a ghost," Richard asked with a concerned look on his face.

"Uh, yes, yes, I'm fine. For a minute, I thought Mr. Maxwell and I had met before, and I was trying to remember where that might have been," she answered with hesitation, trying not to stutter. She could not take her eyes off of George, even though she tried not to stare. She tried to estimate his age and guessed it to be around forty. *Yes, the age was close enough to be right.* She watched as the two men finished their greeting to each other, then quickly took Richard's arm for support.

They were finally escorted by the server to their seats. How could she continue with this meeting and not fall apart? Melinda could feel the emotions beginning to rise in her, and she knew that she would not be able to contain them. *These men will think that I'm crazy, but I have to excuse myself and leave for a few minutes. Now!*

"I'm so sorry, but I need to find the ladies' room," Melinda said as she rose from her chair. The three men rose with her, and George pointed in the direction of the rest rooms. Melinda's legs were weak as she walked to the lounge.

Once inside, she leaned against the wall and was grateful for the chance finally to be alone for a few minutes. The tears streamed down her face uncontrollably and all of the hurt and guilt came flooding back. *After all of these years, is this God's way of punishing me and making me pay for the mistake I made as a young girl? It couldn't be. The God I love would never be so cruel.*

Melinda knew that she had to regain her composure and try to get through this meeting until she could get alone and figure out what to do. She could not fall apart. There was always a chance that she could be mistaken, but George

Maxwell looked just like the man who said he loved her and then broke her heart and left her alone and pregnant.

Melinda had never told Richard about the baby and the adoption when she was a young fifteen year old girl. There was no need; it was long ago. *How can this be?* she screamed within herself as she doubled over and braced herself against the wall. How would she tell him now? And what about George, how much did he know? Did he know his birth name was really Evan Mitchell?

Melinda jumped at the knock on the door.

"Melinda, are you still in there? Are you OK?" Richard asked.

She called out, "Yes, I'll be right out." She looked in the mirror and grabbed a tissue from the complimentary supply to dab her eyes before turning to walk out. Richard was waiting for her on the other side of the door. "I guess I was more nervous than I realized about this meeting. I just got a little queasy, but I'm all right now."

"We can leave if you're not feeling well and do this some other time," Richard offered.

"No, no. I'll be fine," Melinda said with a determined shake of her head. "I want to get through this. I want to hear what, uh, Mr. Maxwell has to say."

Melinda took Richard's arm as they made their way back to the table. She took a deep breath as she fought back her emotions. The other two men rose from their seats as she approached. George Maxwell instinctively stepped forward to help Melinda with her chair as he seated her on his right side. Richard returned to his seat across from George.

"I'm so sorry. I don't know what came over me. I do apologize, Mr. Maxwell," she said facing her host. "It really is so nice that you would take time from your busy day to meet with us personally."

"It's my pleasure, and I hope you're feeling better." George was momentarily distracted as he looked into Melinda's eyes and caught a glimpse of familiarity. Their kindness pierced through his facade. Turning to the others, Maxwell graciously thanked them for agreeing to meet with him and acknowledged his gratitude to Scott for helping to set it up. He offered some recommendations for some of the menu selections and motioned for the waiter to keep the water glasses filled and his guests well served.

Richard finally settled on the blackened tuna sandwich with tequila chili mayonnaise. Scott and George chose the spinach salad with toasted pine nuts, bleu cheese and citrus vinaigrette. Scott's allegiance to Maxwell couldn't have been more obvious. Melinda was certain she'd never be able to eat a bite but didn't want to call any more attention to herself. She finally ordered the Maine lobster salad with citrus aioli.

"Great choices. I'm sure you'll all be pleased," Maxwell explained after the waiter collected their menus and disappeared to turn in their orders. Richard wasn't interested in wasting any time and took George off guard as he quickly changed the subject.

"Mr. Maxwell."

"Please, call me George."

"OK, . . . George," Richard deferred with a slight wave of his hand in his host's direction. "I suggest that we avoid any uncomfortable pauses in conversation and get right to the purpose of this meeting. Scott has provided a few of the details, but he made it clear that you wanted to speak for yourself and on behalf of Global Financial. And, please call us Richard and Melinda."

"Thank you, Richard, for your candor. I believe that's an excellent idea. As you know, Global Financial experienced a loss of customer data last June."

"Yes, we're well aware of that. Our daughter was one of the unfortunate victims," Melinda offered, surprised at the abruptness of her tone.

"Oh? I wasn't aware of that. I hope we've been able to assist her successfully with any consequences," Maxwell replied.

"I believe she's very satisfied with Global's prompt response to her loss," Scott quickly added, a bit too solicitously. Melinda shot him a look that she wished she could have taken back. Scott looked away and turned his attention back to his boss.

George Maxwell detected the slight tension that had surfaced and quickly regained control of the conversation. He acknowledged that he was aware of the protest movement and the Andrews' involvement in its organization. No hard feelings, of course. He tried to portray himself as a man who would never seek to harm his friends or associates with business decisions.

"In fact, I intend to take the embedded chip myself as a good faith gesture . . ."

Melinda froze. It had never even occurred to her that George would receive the mark. She felt her head spinning. She took a deep breath and reached for her water. She quickly put the glass back on the table, her shaking hand having revealed her inner turmoil. *Don't react,* she slowly cautioned herself as she tried to refocus on what George and Richard were saying to each other. Maxwell was giving it his best shot, but it was obvious that Richard wasn't going to back down.

I wonder why Melinda is being so quiet? Scott thought. *It sure isn't like her, although it may be for the best. Things could really get tense.* He was grateful when their lunch arrived. It provided a much needed diversion.

During lunch, George continued to make his pitch to Melinda and Richard. They politely listened and tried to explain their views as well. Maxwell was careful not to appear harsh or heavy handed. He knew he could be intimidating if necessary, but he hoped he would persuade them with sound reasoning instead.

Richard tried to explain their opposition, that for all outward appearances, the microchip might seem like a great technological advancement. But, what about its misuse? Could it be perverted in the hands of a criminal? Or, would it become intrusive and an infringement on civil liberties if at some point it became mandatory? Could Global Financial guarantee those things would not happen?

"Are you saying that you don't have enough trust in humanity to use the embedded chip as it was originally intended?" George asked.

"Well, it wouldn't be the first time that technology was misused, now would it?"

The two men continued with their friendly debate as they finished their lunch. George informed them all that he knew he'd have to convince the protestors from the civil liberties unions as well and that he planned to speak to a representative in the next few days. Scott occasionally joined in with neutral comments, just enough to appear that he was more than the common denominator for each side, although he felt like the stranger in the group.

Melinda silently watched Richard and George as they exchanged ideas. She felt fortunate to be a part of this meeting, to see another side of George that was generally closed to the public. He was charming and smart, well spoken, a born leader. Both sides promised to consider seriously the information that had been exchanged. George even agreed to take a look at Melinda's research, but he was certain it wouldn't change his mind.

During coffee, Melinda finally gathered the courage to get more personal. "George, I noticed the monogram on your cuff, GEM. Mind telling me your middle name?"

"Not at all," he replied. "It's Evan. George Evan Maxwell. My folks had a pretty high opinion of me from the beginning. They called my their little gem. Pretty corny, huh?"

"No, parents are like that. I'm sure you've made them very proud. Are they still alive?"

"No, no, they're not." George raised his cup for a sip of coffee. As he did, he noticed that Melinda was studying his face. He wanted to go on.

"Actually, they were older when they, uh, uh, when I was born, so they've been gone now a few years," George said as he lowered his cup back to the saucer.

Melinda noticed his hesitation to find the right words and decided to push for more details. "Were you born here, or perhaps grow up around here?"

"Yes and no," George said with a smile.

Melinda smiled back, raised her eyebrows and nodded for him to continue. She could barely contain her pleasure when he did.

"I was born in White Plains, but I was adopted as a baby and grew up near Chicago. And, no, I'm not looking for sympathy. I have no anger or bitterness toward my birth mother at all. I had a very pleasant and blessed childhood, good parents, and, so far, I've enjoyed an extraordinary life. I have to believe that my birth mother knew I'd be better off without her." His last comment sent a painful jolt through Melinda, but it was true.

"Have you ever thought about locating her?"

"Not really. My parents told me all about the adoption and even encouraged me to try to get in touch, but I never did. Never needed to. My parents gave me the file before they died in case I ever had any health issues and needed some answers. But, no, it's just never been an issue with me."

Scott and Richard were engaged in their own small talk, but both were keenly aware of the conversation going on between George and Melinda. Scott had never heard the details of Mr. Maxwell's birth and was astonished that he was divulging so much to Melinda, a stranger. He felt like an eavesdropper just sitting at the same table with them.

George, too, was amazed at the freedom he felt to share the events of his childhood. He couldn't remember the last time that he felt so comfortable talking with anyone. Melinda was sincere, and she made him feel completely at ease. What an unexpected turn of events. This meeting was supposed to help him convince the Andrews that he was trustworthy, and his plans for Global Financial were to promote security, that the chip was safe and meant to help. And, most of all, the protesters should all stay home.

Maxwell found himself actually hoping that Melinda would continue to ask about his background. He truly enjoyed their conversation. No one had ever shown this much interest in who he was. People mostly were interested in how much he was worth, what he could do for them, for the bank, for the shareholders.

The dining room began to clear, and it was obvious that the manager was eager to start setting up for the dinner crowd. Maxwell reluctantly brought the meeting to a close but promised he'd call the Andrews in a few days after they'd had an opportunity to consider his request to call off the protest rally.

On the drive home, Melinda slipped into her own thoughts and marveled at the irony of her life. She didn't believe in coincidence or fate. She believed that God was in charge of her life and that the lunch meeting with George Maxwell had been a divine appointment. She and her son had been reunited in a way that only God could have arranged.

Melinda remembered back to the day of his birth and how she reluctantly handed the baby to the nurse and then sobbed on her own mother's shoulder. For years she had refused to allow any bitterness to take root because she knew her son would be all right. Even now, she was grateful for his eventful life, even though she had missed all of it. Even so, Melinda had a peace about her. She had no words to describe how she felt, only a reverent awe of the omniscience of God. *Thank you, Lord, for the good parents whom you provided for my child and the blessings in his life. Now, help me to protect him from this lie and deception. I know that our reunion wasn't a coincidence. Help me to reach him before it's too late. Open his heart to receive me and your Word.*

Melinda could clearly see how God had set all of this in motion, and she knew that she was exactly in the right place and in God's timing. Now one step at a time. She had to tell Richard.

Richard was completely oblivious to the revelation unfolding before them as he summarized the highlights of the meeting. Traffic was not heavy on the drive back to New Rochelle, so he chatted freely and enthusiastically. He thought the meeting had gone well, and he was encouraged that George was sincere when he said he would consider their position. He couldn't help but notice how open Maxwell had been with Melinda about his personal life.

But Melinda stared straight ahead at the traffic as he spoke. She tried to smile and nod as he recounted what he'd overheard of her conversation with George. Yes, George had allowed her in, and she planned to get a lot more personal. Finally, she turned toward her husband and spoke as a tear ran down her cheek. "Richard, there's something really important that I need to tell you."

CHAPTER TWENTY-TWO

They sat and faced each other at the kitchen table just as they'd done hundreds of times before. That table was the gathering place for countless delicious meals, school projects and homework assignments, as well as the family devotions and prayers. Now, it was the place where Richard and Melinda's lives would be changed forever.

Richard waited patiently as Melinda gathered her thoughts and composure. She had wept quietly for the past few minutes and occasionally smiled and shook her head in disbelief. Richard offered her his handkerchief and waited. He couldn't tell for sure if she was about to reveal good news or bad.

"Honey, what is it?" he finally asked, no longer able to contain his curiosity.

"Things have changed, Richard," she began. "This whole protest movement is bigger than we ever realized."

"You're not thinking about quitting, are you?"

"No," she said, as she shook her head emphatically. "It's not that at all."

"Then what? Melinda, you can trust me. I can tell you're distraught. Please tell me."

"Something happened a long time ago when I was a young girl. I never told you because I wanted to put it all behind me. I wanted us to have only each other."

"What are you talking about? I don't understand."

Melinda took a deep breath then slowly exhaled. "When I was fifteen," she started, then raised her eyes and looked straight at Richard. She spoke with soft but deliberate words. "I had a child, a son. His father was tall with dark hair, an athlete's build." She paused again.

"What?" he asked incredulously. "What are you saying?"

"Please, let me finish before I lose my nerve." Melinda took another deep breath and sat up a little straighter. "The baby was born in White Plains where my family and I lived at that time. I gave the child up for adoption to an older couple from Chicago. I named him Evan." Melinda hesitated in order to let her words sink in. Her eyes filled with tears as she looked at Richard for any sign of understanding.

For the next ten minutes, Melinda explained the whole story, how she'd blindly trusted the handsome young man who'd swept her off her feet, then cast her aside when she learned she was pregnant. She spoke with the sweetness of an innocent girl as she recounted the bitter details.

At times, her voice trailed off in uncompleted sentences, and she stared without focusing at nothing in particular as her memory shot back to a particular detail or conversation that had been locked away for more than forty years.

Richard tried to pull her back and encouraged her to continue. "Melinda, I would have understood. Why didn't you tell me before?" he asked compassionately during one of her silences.

Melinda turned her eyes back on him. "I wanted to forget about it. I was hurt and ashamed. It all happened a long time ago, and I thought I'd never have to deal with it again. I'm sorry I never told you. Please, forgive me," she said, sobbing. She buried her face in her hands.

"Honey, there's nothing to forgive. I just wish I could have helped you carry this weight all these years." Richard cupped her chin in his hand and coaxed her face toward him. "So, why are you telling me all of this now?"

Melinda gently blew her nose and took another deep breath. She sat silently and stared down at the table. Finally, she raised her head again and said, "Richard, George Maxwell is the spitting image of the baby's father. I almost couldn't stand up when I first saw him."

Richard didn't speak at first. He looked directly into Melinda's eyes as his mind tried to process what he'd just heard. He felt his eyes slightly twitch and blink as he began to understand. He tried to think of something that he could say that would hide the mixed feelings now swirling inside of him. Finally, he managed to speak.

"Well, at least that explains your behavior at the restaurant. I couldn't figure out what was going on. That little spell came on you so suddenly. I thought you'd taken ill."

"I'm utterly confused, Richard. I don't know what to do. His age fits, and George did say that he was born in White Plains and was adopted by a couple from Chicago. It all fits." Melinda paused and caught her breath, trying to control her emotions. "I can't just ignore this. I really believe that it wasn't a chance meeting or coincidence that our paths crossed."

"No," Richard said slowly as he shook his head. "I would definitely agree. It's not a coincidence." That was an understatement, but Richard's mind was still overwhelmed with his own emotions and reaction to his wife's revelation. He was trying to be supportive, but at the same time grasp the reality that not only had she concealed the existence of another child, but that it was possible they'd all had lunch together that very day. He wasn't certain how he felt about it all. For now though, it wasn't about him. He knew that he needed to be strong for Melinda. He couldn't even imagine what she must be going through.

"I don't know what I'm supposed to do. My secret has come full circle and right back where it all began—with me. But, I can't just pick up the phone and say, 'Thank you so much, Mr. Maxwell for the lovely lunch and your time, and—oh, by the way, I think I'm your mother.'"

"Well, first of all, it's not what you are going to do, it's what *we* are going to do," Richard reassured her. "We're in this together. And, you're right. This has gone way beyond a protest rally, or a new bank card, or an implanted microchip. We seem to be right in the middle of something way beyond anything that we could have ever set up. Honey, you've had quite a day. We need to sleep on it and pray for God's wisdom and direction."

Richard knew he needed time to adjust to this new information, too. But, there was no time. The bank's announcement was only days away. If Melinda was going to reveal the truth to George before then, she'd have to move quickly. And, they had to tell Jacob and Sarah, no more secrets. And what about their friends and all of the volunteers helping with the protest? What would they tell them?

Warm tears eased down Melinda's face, and her shoulders softly shook as she released each sob. In the midst of it, Melinda felt peace come over her. Her deepest secret from her past was finally uncovered, and she felt free. She knew she'd have to tell George. He had a right to know. Thankfully, God was in control, and they were all just along for the ride. There was one thing for certain she did know: she didn't want to miss a single minute.

CHAPTER TWENTY-THREE

Although Melinda tried, she couldn't sleep. She was restless and couldn't get comfortable. Her mind just wouldn't shut down. She tried to imagine what she would say to George Maxwell if he agreed to schedule another meeting with her. And how would she even ask him to meet? What could she possibly say that would get his attention, enough for him to give up even more of his time? He wasn't a man who had time to spare. The bank's announcement day was fast approaching; Maxwell's thoughts and attention were elsewhere.

Not wanting to disturb Richard, Melinda finally got up and went to the kitchen to fix some coffee. It was obvious that she was going to be up all night anyway, she may as well enjoy a good pot of coffee.

Melinda held the warm cup between her hands and blew across the top of the liquid as she went back in time to a place long ago. After the unexpected pregnancy and betrayal, she had promised herself she'd never again be so naive. She would never allow anyone else to take such advantage of her emotions or her trusting nature. She'd promised herself she wouldn't get bogged down by guilt and regret and that she'd move on, a little wiser. And she had. Her family had relocated to New Rochelle for a fresh start. They were amazed and delighted at how quickly Melinda recovered from her broken heart and the rejection of the young man. Her mother was pleased to see Melinda start to mature and focus on her new school and friends. They all thought they'd left her secret in White Plains.

Now, Melinda simply would not allow herself to second guess her decision about the adoption, and she quickly forced any shadow of regret from her mind. The announcement and protest rally were one week away. She had chosen to remove Evan from her life more than forty years ago and had resigned herself to the fact that he belonged to another family. Yet, here he was, as George Maxwell, less that an hour away. Did she really owe him anything? He'd said himself that he had no regrets, that he'd had a good life, that he wasn't bitter. Maybe it would be better to just leave things as they were.

Numerous options raced through her mind. She could feel the inner conflict tearing at her heart. *Why didn't you ever tell Richard or the children? Were you afraid they'd think less of you, so the less they knew, the better? Did it make you feel better not to deal with your secret? To try to bury it long ago? Are you going to continue to pretend that you don't have another son so you don't have to deal with it now?*

No, Melinda trusted God, and only he could have orchestrated this chain of events. If God was in it, she had nothing to fear. She must deal with the truth now. She had to face it head on and make the right choice. No more running. No more pretending.

She knew that Richard would never betray her confidence or tell anyone unless she agreed, but the hidden past always would be an unspoken and unseen wedge between them. Richard always would wonder if there was more she'd never told him. She knew what she must do.

She had to find the courage to tell her children, including George Maxwell, the truth. But how? It would change things forever. Their lives would never be the same. And the timing of the truth was now urgent. George was planning to promote the new banking technology that she feared was the precursor of an economic system linked to the mark of the Beast. Once again, as she had throughout the night, Melinda buried her face in her hands and cried out to God.

Melinda looked around her chair. She counted at least six pieces of paper that had been wadded up and tossed on the floor. Every time she'd tried to put her thoughts on paper, there were so many crossed out words and arrows darting from one sentence to another, she couldn't follow what she had written. It was almost dawn now, and the caffeine was wearing off. The lack of sleep was taking its toll, and it was difficult for Melinda to focus. Still, she had to get something down on paper, and get it in the mail today. Time was running out. Melinda picked up her pen and tried once more.

Dear Mr. Maxwell: Melinda crossed out "Mr. Maxwell" and substituted "George."

Dear George:

It was a genuine pleasure joining you for lunch. Thank you for your hospitality and time. I know you are very busy, so it was especially kind of you to agree to meet with us.

I am enclosing a copy of our research about the mark of the Beast and the original Greek text used in the book of Revelation. I hope you will carefully read all of the information with an open mind.

Richard and I have considered your request to cancel the protest rally, but we must decline. We feel very strongly that the Lord has directed us to do this, so we must.

It was very special of you to share some of the details of your personal life with me. I would love to speak with you some more about your birth and adoption. I have some information that I would like to share with you. I'll be waiting for your call, if you're interested.

Sincerely,
Melinda Andrews

There. I don't know what else to say, so I'm just going to send this before I change my mind or lose my nerve. Melinda hesitated before sealing the envelope. *Maybe I should have Richard look at it, see what he thinks.* She quickly shook her head and licked the flap. *No. I'm going with my first impression and trust that it says the right thing.*

CHAPTER TWENTY-FOUR

George Maxwell's eyes narrowed, and he furrowed his brow as he re-read the personal thank-you note from Melinda Andrews that had come in the morning mail. He wasn't all that surprised at the first part, where she let him know that they were going forward with the protest, but he was taken back by the last paragraph. Why did she want to talk about his birth again? The note said she had "information." What kind of information? What an unusual request. What could she possibly know?

George frowned as he dropped the paper on his desk. He had a morning full of meetings. He surely didn't have any spare time for casual chit chat with a woman who was hell-bent on stirring up negative publicity about him and his bank. Still, the hook was set.

After his lunch meeting with Richard and Melinda a few days ago, George knew as sure as he knew his own name that the Andrews had not been persuaded to back down from their protest. Even so, he had enjoyed their meeting, and he knew they weren't acting out of malice toward him or Global Financial. They had their convictions, and he had his. George glanced at his calendar for the day. *Well, I guess I could spare five minutes.*

George reached for his intercom button. "Helen, see if you can find the phone number for Richard and Melinda Andrews in New Rochelle. Ask Scott Spencer. He'll probably have it."

"Yes, sir, Mr. Maxwell. Would you like for me to place the call for you?"

"Uh, no. I'll do it myself."

Fifteen minutes later, as George pushed the numbers on his telephone key pad, he still was puzzled by Melinda's obvious lure for him to call. After three rings, Melinda answered.

"George, I am so glad you called." Melinda fought to remain calm as the anxiety begin to creep in.

"I hope it's not too early."

"Oh, no, not at all. I know how busy you are, and I really appreciate that you would take the time."

"Well, yes, things are pretty hectic right now. But I must admit, I am curious as to what you meant about having information you'd like to share about my birth."

Melinda laughed nervously. "I hope my note didn't sound too mysterious. It's just . . . well, it's um . . . I have something that should be discussed with you directly, even if it is over the phone. It's not something I'd write in a thank-you note."

"Well, I'm afraid that I don't have much time for the next few days. As you can imagine, we're running on a tight schedule trying to get ready for the big day. Can it wait for a couple of weeks until I'm not so busy?"

"Uh, well, . . . no. It really can't. Well, uh, . . . actually it really shouldn't. So, uh, I guess I'll just get right to the point and tell you now." Melinda took an audible deep breath and exhaled into the phone. She summonsed all of her courage, prayed silently to God, and continued. "Um, you said that you had a folder with your adoption paperwork that your parents left you." She spoke slowly and deliberately in hope of controlling her voice.

"Yes," George hesitated. "It's with my personal files at home. Why?"

"Well, have you ever looked at your birth mother's name?" Melinda's voice trembled.

"Yes," George answered cautiously. "I've looked at the whole file, but it was such a long time ago, that I don't recall that much about it," he lied. Actually, he'd read and studied the entire contents several times and committed the information to memory in case he ever had any health issues that traced back to his birth mother's medical history. He wasn't certain where this conversation was headed, so he waited for Melinda to continue.

She spoke with hesitation. "Do you recall if your mother's last name was 'Mitchell?'"

She had George's attention now. *How could this woman possibly know his birth mother's name? He'd never told anyone about the contents of the adoption file.* "That sounds familiar. I'd have to check to be sure, but may I ask why?" He felt his pulse quicken as he waited for Melinda's response.

Melinda's heart pounded. She felt light-headed. Her eyes filled with tears. She tried, but failed, to speak with a steady voice. Finally, she was able to say, barely above a whisper, "I was Melinda Mitchell." There was no response on the other end of the line, so she continued, a little bolder, "Melinda Mitchell, from White Plains, New York."

It was the first time in his life George Maxwell ever remembered being absolutely speechless.

CHAPTER TWENTY-FIVE

George Maxwell willed himself to concentrate on his day's agenda. He had no choice. He must put Melinda's phone call out of his mind until he could get alone to think and fully comprehend its impact. Global Financial was heading into one of its milestone weeks with the unveiling of the embedded microchip technology and the new bank card.

The bank's marketing department had already spent millions in advertising. A dozen East Coast newspapers were running full page announcements of the event for the next five days. All of the major television networks and cable news channels were covering the story. Maxwell was pushing hard to get them to run a trailer at the bottom of the screen all during the nightly news program with the details of how and where to get chipped.

George Maxwell was the youngest President, Chairman of the Board and CEO in Global Financial's history. He was its leader. He would take Global Financial Bank into this new realm of banking, and he would not fail. He couldn't indulge in even the slightest of a distraction, much less the bombshell Melinda had just dropped on him.

All day he had meetings with several bank officers for the last minute briefings about preparations for the upcoming announcement. He had to review the final draft of the brochure that was going out to the bank's customers and give his approval. He had a lunch meeting with Elizabeth Hume to go over the contract between Global Financial Bank and Applied Digital Solutions one last time. He wanted to ensure he was very familiar with the terms and conditions in case he had to answer any questions next week. He had to peruse the latest newspaper articles and letters to the editors from all of the supporters and protestors. One thing for sure, the new bank card and imbedded bank chip were getting lots of publicity, good and bad, and George Maxwell had to be prepared for anything.

At the end of the day, George finally saw his chance to get alone and think. The phones had stopped ringing, and the corridors and offices were empty. He gathered up some notes and files and dropped them into his briefcase to read later that evening. He called for Reese to bring the limo around to take him home.

On the drive uptown to his lush surroundings in Carnegie Hill, Maxwell finally let his mind wander back to the early morning phone call with Melinda Andrews and her shocking revelation.

"George, I am truly sorry to come into your life like this and so abruptly." She could tell he'd been shaken, and she tried to soften the impact. "I can't even imagine how you must feel."

"Well, I'm not really sure how I feel. This is quite a shock."

"It's pretty mind-boggling for me as well, and I've tried to figure out the best way to handle all of this. I'm still not sure."

"I don't know what to say. I need to think about this." He measured his comments. "You weren't kidding when you said you had some information. How long have you known?"

"Only since our conversation at lunch yesterday after you confirmed some of my suspicions." Richard remained silent, so Melinda nervously filled in the silence. "I truly believe that the way these events have unfolded, there has to be some sort of divine intervention. There has to be a reason for us to meet after all of this time."

Against his better judgment, he asked, "Such as?"

"I'm asking you . . . no, I am begging you. Please, don't go through with this plan. Please, don't let anyone inject that chip under your skin."

She went on and on about her reasons and beliefs. He was still too stunned to contribute much to the conversation. George was tempted to hang up on her, to end this intrusion into his life. Already he'd allowed her far too much familiarity. Instead, he found himself wanting to talk more, to gather more information. As she continued to explain her concerns, he felt a flash of déjà vu that sent a shiver all through him.

Finally, he spoke up. "So, are you saying that you believe that I'm going to be condemned forever if I take the new bank chip? That I'm going to align myself with the Antichrist?"

"No. I'm not saying that at all. I can't even say for sure that the embedded microchip is the mark of the Beast. But, if not, I believe it's the precursor to it." Melinda had found her voice again and spoke with confidence. "It's like the fingerprint and iris scans used at airports for access to a special screening lane and a quicker pass through security. Or the use of a fingerprint at the grocery store for a faster checkout, or a national ID card using biometric data. All of these so called conveniences are marketed as protections for greater security and safety. And, the American public is being seduced into believing that this new technology actually makes us safer. But, it doesn't. We're not safer. We just have more sophisticated toys, so we think we're safer. But, only God can protect us."

"Melinda, you don't understand. I have to go through with this plan," George said finally cutting in. "I'm the one who pushed it through to the board of directors and to two other bank presidents, who pushed it through to their directors. I assured them that the VeriChip was state of the art in banking. Now, you're telling me that it's a precursor to the mark of the Beast? Do you know how ridiculous that sounds?" George tried not to sound too harsh.

Melinda felt her courage fade again and didn't even try to refute him. George ended the phone call by promising Melinda he'd review his adoption papers when he got the chance and try to get back with her soon. He already knew what the papers said. He just didn't know what he was going to do about it. Another first.

Reese pulled the limousine up to the curb in front of Maxwell's building. He jumped out to help Mr. Maxwell with his door.

"Thanks, Reese. I'll see you first thing in the morning. Sorry I'm not very good company."

"Yes, sir, Mr. Maxwell. I'll be here. Have a nice evening, sir."

Maxwell walked briskly through the entrance of the lobby to the waiting elevators. Inside, he tried to collect his thoughts and concentrate on his next move. George stepped out of the elevator directly into his luxurious penthouse suite. He placed his briefcase on the large mahogany table with an inlaid imported marble top and punched in the security code to disarm the alarm. On a mission now, George headed straight to his study, to the left of the foyer, where he kept his personal files. The adoption papers were in the bottom drawer of the file cabinet in a small accordion folder.

At first, he fumbled with the small key. Finally, he was able to steady his hand and open the drawer. As he lifted the brown folder out of the compartment, he noticed that beads of sweat had formed on his forehead and that his hands had become clammy. *George, what are you doing? You've left this folder buried in this drawer and in your past for most of your adult life. Leave it alone.*

But he couldn't leave it alone. He hadn't admitted it to Melinda during their telephone conversation, but he, too, had felt swept into this tidal wave, this collision course with destiny, as soon as he'd stepped into St. Maggie's Café for lunch with the Andrews. For a reason he couldn't explain, the minute he shook Melinda's hand and they exchanged their pleasantries, he was drawn to her. She had made him feel completely comfortable during their conversation. Her voice had been soothing, and there had been something inexplicably familiar about her.

It had always sounded corny to him that twins, who'd been separated at birth, instinctively sought out an identical lifestyle and career as the other. And, George had heard about cases of adopted children who'd spent years trying to find their birth parents, or at least their mothers, just to ask, "Why?" Even though they were strangers, their shared blood drew them together like magnets. He never understood it. It wouldn't change anything as far as George was concerned, so he didn't care. Why couldn't his past reciprocate and just leave him alone?

George quickly sorted through the papers in the folder until he found his record of birth. Even though he'd read it before and knew what it said, this time it wasn't just bare statistics. This time the name had a face. This time there was a connection.

He stared at the boxes across the top of the page. "Evan Mitchell, white male, eight pounds, twenty-one inches, born to Melinda Mitchell, white female, age 15, White Plains, New York. Father unlisted."

George lowered the paper and sat down at his desk. He drew in a deep breath, leaned back in his chair, and turned to face the windows for a panoramic view of the city. Across the street, to the west, was Central Park. George could see the park's lights flickering through the new leaves that had opened during the past two weeks. To outsiders, Central Park was a place to avoid. It was infamous for the assaults and robberies against the weak and unwary. Years ago, the news headlines shocked the nation when an attractive young woman, out for her daily jog through the park, was beaten and gang raped in broad daylight and left for dead.

But to the residents of Manhattan, Central Park was a sanctuary, a place to escape from the pressures of the day. It was a place to enjoy the beauty of all forms of nature, not a destination to fear.

There were no words to describe springtime in Manhattan. The trees were radiant against the blue sky. The soft hues and sweet fragrances of the blossoms overwhelmed the senses like an intoxicant. Every year the natives and tourists made their pilgrimage to Central Park to celebrate and welcome the re-birth of nature. And every year the crowds proclaimed that Central Park was more beautiful than they'd ever remembered.

Though daylight was fading, the park would still be alive with joggers and walkers and pets trying to squeeze in every last minute before giving up the day. But George was not one of them. Not today. This particular evening, in the final days of spring when others were honoring the rites of the season, George Maxwell sat quietly in his study in his opulent penthouse suite with his birth statistics in his hand, oblivious the strangers in the distance. He felt numb. *So, who are you, really?* he challenged himself.

Earlier that day, Melinda Andrews had revealed the truth of her past and their connection. She'd asked him to abandon his plans to take the embedded chip and to cancel the event at the bank so that others wouldn't be exposed to any potential harm. She hadn't asked him to do these things as his mother. She'd wisely realized that she had relinquished that privilege long ago and would now sound trite if she tried to play that card. No, she'd asked him as . . . what was it she'd called herself? A "believer." Yes, that was it. She was a believer. She was a believer who worried that George was on a dangerous path and would influence others to follow him.

She had conceded it was unlikely that the embedded chip was the actual mark of the Beast, more like a precursor. So, what was the harm? He'd be careful and watchful now that she'd made him aware of its potential misuse. He was a smart and well-educated man. He knew better than to make careless, snap decisions. So, of course he knew better than to worship or to vow an allegiance to a "Beast." He just didn't see why the new technology was such a big deal.

George looked at the paper in his hand and then back out his window to the skyline and down to the streets of Manhattan. The street lights were brighter now as darkness closed in on the city. George posed the question again and then answered with subdued determination. *Who am I really? I'm George Evan Maxwell, President, Chairman of the Board, and CEO of Global Financial Bank.*

CHAPTER TWENTY-SIX

The long awaited day had almost arrived. It was just twenty-four hours away. George Maxwell was pleased with his colleagues and staff, their preparation, and about the big event planned for tomorrow. Once again, under his leadership, Global Financial Bank was in the headlines as the pioneer of 21st century banking. And everything was in place to usher in the big day. In fact, they were ahead of schedule.

George sat at his desk, then swiveled his chair around so he could see the Manhattan skyline, and reflect on the past twelve months. It would be a year ago tomorrow since the chain of events had begun that had forced the bank's need for greater protection against identity theft. June 6, 2005, had been a wake-up call for Global Financial and the entire banking industry to the fact that thieves were smarter than any software firewall or secure computer database. The industry had to respond and demonstrate it was addressing the problem.

In the last year New York had joined a growing list of states that now required banks and companies to notify their customers whose personal information may have been acquired by an unauthorized person. Security breach victims were becoming a strong lobbying group. The pressure they were putting on American companies for greater security was having a far-reaching effect. The victims represented the voice of consumer and public consciousness. George Maxwell and Global Financial Bank were listening.

But there was another voice also vying for George's attention. And no matter how hard he tried, he could not silence it. *George, I am begging you, please, don't go through with this plan.*

George had intentionally kept people at a safe distance all of his adult life. He had hundreds, thousands of acquaintances, even a few friends in a very loose definition of the word. He had business colleagues and associates and personal domestic employees. But he had been an only child, and after the death of his parents, he rarely kept in touch with any of his aunts or uncles back in Illinois. By his own choice, George was alone.

He didn't know how he was supposed to feel about the sudden appearance of Melinda Andrews in his life. He didn't know why, after all of this time, they unexpectedly had discovered each other. Neither one had been searching. It had just happened. Melinda was certain that God had a hand in it. He still wasn't convinced. Sometimes things just happened.

It bothered him that he couldn't stop thinking about their conversation. He should be feeling elated. He should be enjoying the anticipation of tomorrow and all of the planned festivities. Instead, he felt conflicted. Why?

"I'm going out for a while, Helen."

"Yes, sir. You want me to call for Reese?"

"No." George's tone was grim. He shook his head as he spoke and kept his eyes lowered. "I need to walk." George entered the express elevator to the ground floor and pushed the button for the lobby. He stepped out of the elevator and headed toward the front revolving door and the fresh air of the outside. The sky was cloudless. It was a beautiful, clear day in the city. The air was invigorating against his face. George filled his lungs. *This feels good. Maybe it'll help clear my head.*

George put his hands in his pockets and walked west toward Broadway and Church Street and Ground Zero. He picked up his pace as he slid in step with the morning commuters coming out of the subway stairs onto the busy side streets. Once at the World Trade Center site, George stood alone and stared down into the pit where the towers had once stood. The daily tourists hadn't yet arrived, so George was alone at the sanctuary.

The twin towers of the World Trade Center, once a world symbol of commerce and capitalism, were now gone due to an act of pure evil. George recalled the morning of the terrorists' attack. The sky had been clear and cloudless just like today. People had gone about their morning routines completely oblivious to the evil plans that had been carefully orchestrated and were unfolding that day. He could still envision the twin towers silhouetted against the clear blue sky. Once the tallest buildings in Manhattan, they had dominated the city's skyline.

He could still hear the incessant emergency sirens that echoed off of the buildings for most of the day. He could still smell the thick toxic smoke that filled the air after the first tower had collapsed. It continued to smolder for days and weeks after the attack. He could still envision all of the people wearing white masks to cover their noses and mouths so they could breathe.

He thought back to the nation's collective mentality before the towers had fallen and the Pentagon had been hit that September morning in 2001. Americans thought they were safe—untouchable. They'd been shocked as they had watched their television screens and had seen the live destruction in New York City and Washington, D. C. They were shocked that the World Trade Center had been hit and destroyed. They were shocked that their enemy had used their own planes as deadly weapons against them. They were shocked at the panic that started engulfing the nation. But, most of all, they were shocked that it had happened on their own soil, in their own backyard. *Could it have been avoided?* George wondered as he surveyed the area. *Could we have protected ourselves? Probably not. An enemy without a conscience can't be restrained or predicted.*

Evil had permeated the nation's borders and had spread just like the billowing debris and toxins that had boiled around the collapsing towers and the surrounding streets. Buildings didn't fall just in lower Manhattan that day. They didn't leave a massive pit just in New York City. No, the whole nation had suffered a gaping wound and had been forced to realize its vulnerability.

George looked around at all that was left where the towers once stood. *Before the attack, we thought we were safe. Yet . . .* He let his thought hang unfinished. He had speculated that if he came to this site it would encourage him and renew his belief that he'd find a solution to help others feel secure again.

Instead, he felt inadequate. *How do I overcome a thief with no conscience, no morals, no empathy for others?*

George slowly turned and faced St. Paul's Chapel across the street. He recalled how in the midst of the smoldering fire and debris, of the destruction and calamity and unspeakable horror, that the bells of St. Paul's rang out as if to announce that God was still ever present and still in control. George looked back at the pit, then slid his hands back into his pockets and walked to the corner to cross the street. He needed to do something that he hadn't done in a very long time.

CHAPTER TWENTY-SEVEN

St. Paul's Chapel was completed in 1766 on what was then the northern edge of the city. It was constructed of Manhattan mica-schist with brownstone quoins. All of its carvings, door hinges, and woodwork were handmade.

Over the altar was an ornamental design of the "Glory," the work of Pierre L'Enfant who also had designed Washington D.C. "The Glory" depicted Mt. Sinai in clouds and lightning, the two tablets bearing the Ten Commandments, and the Hebrew word for "God."

George Washington attended a special prayer service at St. Paul's Chapel after his inauguration on April 30, 1789. He continued to worship there during the two years that New York City served as the nation's capital. An oil painting of the first rendition of the Great Seal of the United Stated still hung above his pew. In 1799, a memorial service was held for Washington in the chapel.

St. Paul's Chapel remained as the only surviving church of the Revolutionary era in New York and served as the oldest public building in continuous use in Manhattan. Miraculously, it stood undamaged, despite being directly across the street when the twin towers collapsed. There wasn't so much as a single broken window.

Even though there was no phone service or electricity for days, St. Paul's Chapel served as a gathering point for the firefighters and emergency crews at the former World Trade Center site. For eight months, the chapel functioned as a place of refuge. It was a place for the recovery workers to find rest and consolation. It was a place for the weary and homeless to find food and a bed. It was a place for the downtrodden to find counseling and prayer. It was a place for recovering spiritually.

George Maxwell quietly opened the heavy front door and stepped in. He made his way into the sanctuary and slipped into one of the rear pews on the far left side. The chapel was empty and still. He walked lightly on the hard floor so as not to break the solitude and calm. Once inside, the sidewalk noise was completely silenced. It was a stark contrast to the scene the city had witnessed on September 11 and the days that followed.

Besides the horrific image of the planes deliberately crashing into the World Trade Center and the pandemonium that followed, the most vivid memory George had of that day was the dust that had settled over lower Manhattan. Dust was on everything, everywhere. Six inches of ash covered the streets. It provided an eerie gray shroud that connected the area for blocks. One hardly knew where to start cleaning first.

As George sat quietly in the pew and reflected on the memory of the dust and how it enveloped everything, his mind wandered back to a scene from years ago. He was at his father's grave. He recalled the Scriptures that were read as the casket was lowered into the ground. "And the Lord God formed man of the dust of the ground and breathed into his nostrils the breath of life; and man became a living soul. For dust thou art, and unto dust shalt thou return."

George Maxwell smiled and gently shook his head as he considered the irony. *Just think of how much time and money we spend trying to rid our daily lives of dust. We judge a person's housekeeping abilities by the presence of dust. Nosy visitors feel compelled to inspect a bookshelf or windowsill. We grab a broom or dust cloth at any sign of it. Yet, the Scriptures tell us that our origin is the dust of the ground.*

George opened his eyes and looked around at the beauty of St. Paul's. He was relieved that the chapel was still empty and he could enjoy the moment alone. He rose from his seat and walked over to a side window to look out on the churchyard cemetery.

There were numerous patriots who'd served under Washington, as well as some of the early founders of New York City buried at St. Paul's. To the ghosts of the past he whispered, "We're all just dust." With all that the revolutionary heroes had faced and accomplished in the formation of this new country, in the end . . . *What a sobering thought. God picked them to use for His purpose, and now they're just dust.*

At that exact moment, George Maxwell realized how insignificant he was. But, like so many others, he had been seduced by power and blinded by his own self-worth. He'd learned to go about his daily business confident in his own abilities, ignoring the goodness and protections of God. He'd long forgotten and abandoned the promise he'd made to his parents to live by the lessons of his youth.

He'd come to St. Paul's Chapel to try to reconnect to the person his parents had reared, to try to find answers to the conflicting voices that pulled at him. He'd come in hope that the answers would be made clear to him, and he could silence the competing forces. But, once inside, he realized that he was only looking for a quick fix, and that God only wrote messages on a wall or appeared in a burning bush in Bible stories. George couldn't remember the last time he'd prayed. He wasn't even sure he remember how. But he'd always been pretty good with words and surely the Almighty would understand if he was a little out of practice. So, he bowed his head and spoke from his heart.

God, what am I going to do? I've set this plan in motion. I've hailed it as the answer to all of the security problems. I can't now say, "Never mind." The board of directors will demand an explanation, and I don't have one that they'll accept. I've allowed Global Financial Bank to become my life and left You out of all of my decisions. I've boasted of my own accomplishments. I guess I'm asking You for help. What's the answer? Is the chip dangerous? Am I making a bad decision?

George was interrupted by the noise of the first tourists coming in the front door. It was time for him to go. Time to get back to work. As he headed toward the exit, he paused to glance one last time at Washington's pew.

He wondered if George Washington ever sat there, not only to worship, but to seek answers and guidance on how to lead the young nation—how to protect it from enemies foreign and domestic? He wondered if George Washington ever felt that he was personally responsible for the safety of its people. He wondered if God ever spoke to George Washington and gave him answers so he'd know what to do. George Maxwell took a deep breath and slowly exhaled. *I need an answer now because I don't see how I have any choice but to go forward with the plan.*

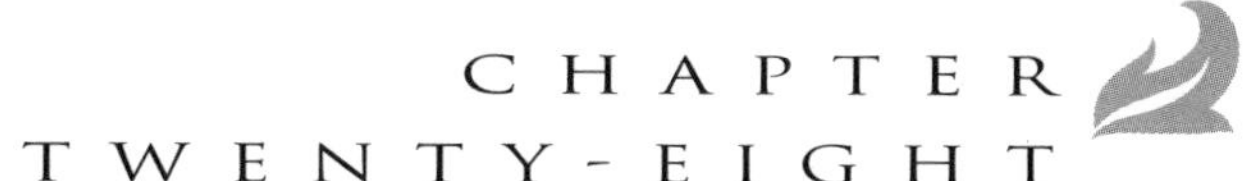

CHAPTER TWENTY-EIGHT

In the 18th, 19th and early 20th centuries, a half dozen streets in the downtown East River shipping district were the original inlets. They were carved into the southern tip of Manhattan where ships arrived with their cargo. In 1934, many of these slips, as they were also known, were filled in and paved as part of the construction along the East River Drive, now named Franklin D. Roosevelt Drive. One of these inlets in particular, Old Slip, was preserved at Water Street and William Street, next to the historic Police Museum building, which served as the New York Police Department's First Precinct station house.

In 2004, as part of the Parks and Recreation Department's restoration project, Old Slip Park was built. Granite curbs, pigmented pavement, decorative benches and well-manicured shrubs and shade trees were added. The park was fittingly designed into the shape of a police badge.

Old Slip Park was a welcome patch of green nestled between the skyscrapers shooting up from the asphalt and concrete. It provided a peaceful place for tourists to enjoy a rest from sightseeing and for the thousands of workers in the surrounding businesses to enjoy a quiet lunch or afternoon break. Old Slip Park was located just a few blocks from the New York Stock Exchange and Wall Street.

On June 6, 2006, it was a gathering place for the protestors to congregate before making their way to Federal Hall to witness Global Financial's announcement of its new banking plans. Melinda and Richard arrived at 7:00 AM to greet the others and be available to assist with any last minute details and to hand out the information flyers to the people on their way to work in the area.

There was a slight breeze from the West, and the sky was overcast. The morning weather announcer predicted rain and alerted the listeners of a severe storm watch in the area. Melinda hoped that the protestors wouldn't decide to stay home because of the warning. She wasn't disappointed.

Around 8:00 AM, the park began to fill up quickly. Melinda estimated that at least two hundred twenty-five protestors had arrived. She recognized several of the people from the numerous informational meetings she and Richard had attended during the past few months. Many of them had taken a vacation day from work just to be here.

Some brought placards. They started their march around the perimeter with their posters held high as soon as they reached the park. Their messages and chanting urged the people hurrying by to refuse the new banking technology. They warned of its connection to the future mark of the Beast.

SAY NO TO THE CHIP! USE MONEY, NOT MARKS! REFUSE THE MARK!

The hustle and commotion of the crowd starting to form provided a much needed distraction for Melinda. She couldn't stop thinking of George and wondering if he'd looked at his adoption file yet. He hadn't yet contacted her. She wondered if her plea had had any impact on him at all. She'd had been up most of last night praying that her son would find the courage to reject the chip and stop the announcement at Federal Hall this morning.

She recalled the early morning hours as she had paced the floor or stared out into the darkness. She once again recognized the overwhelming sense of urgency to publically oppose the bank's plan that she had felt during the last several months. She knew for certain that she had no choice but to follow through with this protest, even though George had requested otherwise. Still, she wondered whether this demonstration through the streets of downtown Manhattan really would do any good. Would the people care or would they just walk away? Would they be too busy or uninterested to pay attention?

The citizens and workers of lower Manhattan who had witnessed first hand and survived the September 11th catastrophe had experienced the most horrific peace-time attack in the history of the nation. The ordeal had made them tough and not easily alarmed. Technological advancements that could make their lives safer or provide more convenience would probably be welcomed. *Oh, Lord, if we only reach one, I feel I must do this,* she had vowed as the dawn had broken earlier that morning.

Melinda pulled her attention back to the present. She looked at her watch and motioned to Richard that it was time to get started; the live news report was scheduled for 9:00 AM. Richard helped get the crowd's attention. Melinda stood on one of the park benches and waved for them to gather in around her.

"OK, guys, listen up. Remember, we are not trying to force this on anybody. If they don't want any of the flyers or to stop and listen, then that's their choice. We are here for those who have ears to hear, not to preach to anyone or tell them that they are doomed. I believe God simply wants us to be in place for those who are open and who will listen."

Some of the pedestrians and a few of the early morning tourists momentarily paused on the sidewalk to listen. Melinda collected her thoughts and continued.

"No doubt, we will face some opposition, but we must meet it with peace. If some people reject our message, that's their choice." She raised her voice and spoke with boldness. "We are here for God, and He will direct us." Cheers and shouts of "Hallelujah" erupted throughout the crowd.

"Be mindful of your actions and be respectful of others' rights to disagree with us. We won't reach many people if we're disruptive and try to force our beliefs on them," Melinda said as she smiled in the direction of a middle-aged woman who was making an obscene gesture in the direction of the protestors.

The group was enthusiastic now and ready to start. Richard and Melinda opened the packages of the flyers that had been prepared to circulate as the protestors walked to Federal Hall. The handouts contained the warning of Revelation 13: 15–18 and a picture of someone being injected with the VeriChip. For special emphasis, the number 666 was at the bottom of each flyer in large bold print.

"OK, we need at least four people at every street corner in a three block square to distribute these," Richard explained. "Any volunteers?"

Several hands shot up, and the bundles of flyers were quickly dispersed. Dozens of people headed in all directions in search of anyone who'd accept the information or stand still long enough to discuss it. Others remained in the park to greet the masses as they walked by on their way to work.

Melinda stopped for a few minutes and watched her friends from church as they spoke with some curious people who had caught a glimpse of the commotion and stopped for more information. Some of them smiled and nodded as they listened. Others stared blankly or furrowed their brows in disbelief at what they heard. Most of the people offered a perfunctory smile and shook their head as they quickly passed in hope of avoiding any proselytizing. They were on their way to work and didn't care or want to be bothered. They were accustomed to the unusual; nothing surprised them.

Melinda's eyes filled with tears and her heart ached as she watched the majority of people turn their heads and hurry past, trying to ignore and avoid the protestors. *Oh, people, please open your eyes and ears. This is real,* she silently begged.

Out of the corner of her eye, she noticed a small group of police officers making their way to the four corners of the park. She wanted to walk over and assure them there would be no violence but decided they'd see for themselves. To her left, she saw two buses pull around the corner and come to a stop on the north side of the park. As the passengers stepped off each bus, she saw they also carried protest signs denouncing the embedded chip, but for a different reason. To her surprise, the local leaders and several members of the New York Civil Liberties Union had arrived to join the rally.

Their posters warned that the computer chip infringed on individual privacy rights and expanded the scope of Big Brother. Melinda waved and smiled at the newcomers. She marveled at the unlikelihood that these two groups would ever find common ground for a protest. *Nothing is impossible with God!* she thought.

"Honey, it's time to start making our way to Federal Hall," Richard said from behind.

Melinda jumped. "Oh, you startled me. I was taking it all in and got lost in thought."

"Sorry. But you're probably a little extra jittery. This isn't exactly a typical day for us," he teased.

"Yes, I'm amazed. Just look at this. It's certainly a lot different from our quiet streets in New Rochelle."

Richard surveyed all of the activity going on in the park. "Well, you did it," he said with an admiring look at his wife.

"Who would have ever thought?" Melinda smiled and slowly shook her head. "Can you believe it? This all started at our kitchen table. Now, here we are almost three hundred strong, and with a police escort to Federal Hall!"

"Yes, and," he said checking his watch, "we're going to miss the whole thing if we don't get going. "I'll get everyone together. Keep your cell phone on in case we get separated."

As the group lined up and prepared to walk, one of the officers at the perimeter of the park blew his whistle. The chanting stopped, and the crowd turned to listen.

"Ladies and gentlemen," the officer began after the crowd quieted. "We can't stop you from protesting, but we can stop you if you break the law. So far, everything has been peaceful, and we expect you to keep it that way. Security is tight around Wall Street, and you will need to stay in the section that has been reserved to the left of the steps at Federal Hall. Let's keep this orderly. No one needs to go to jail today, OK?"

As he spoke, the other police officers made their way to their patrol cars and turned on their flashing lights. One drove to the front of the crowd and slowly began to lead them through the side streets. Another followed the group at the rear.

Melinda felt the tension mounting with every step. Each group of protestors was convinced of the propriety of its position. The volume of their chants increased, and it seemed as if their numbers gained along the way. Maybe people were curious and wanted to see what was stirring such a debate.

From a distance, Melinda saw the steps of Federal Hall. She could make out a temporary platform that had been erected at the base of the steps. Ferns and other greenery flanked the speaker's podium in the center of the platform. She guessed there were about fifty chairs that had been set out for the invited guests and dignitaries.

To her surprise, there were additional police officers positioned between the stage and the space reserved for the guests and the protestors. Security guards stood on the alert in front of the New York Stock Exchange. *Surely, they don't think we're going to get violent or destroy anything.*

So far, all had gone as planned. The rally had been peaceful, but noticeable. Melinda had done the best she knew how to do. She and Richard and the others had hoped they'd be heard. Now, the rest was up to God.

CHAPTER TWENTY-NINE

Federal Hall is prominently located on Wall Street and sits among downtown skyscrapers and other historical landmarks. In 1700, the original structure was built to serve as New York's City Hall. In October 1765, delegates from the original colonies met there for the first time as an organized body to oppose the levying of the Stamp Act by King George III. After the American Revolution the building was remodeled and expanded.

On March 4, 1789, the first United States Congress met at Federal Hall to establish a new government under the Constitution. Its first official order of business was to tally the votes that elected George Washington as the first American president. He was inaugurated in front of the building the following month. A bronze statue of his likeness marked the site on the front steps. The Bible that he used to swear his oath of office was displayed inside.

After the United States capital was moved to Philadelphia in 1790, what had been Federal Hall was again used for New

York City government offices until 1812 when the building was razed. The current structure was built as the nation's first United States Customs House, and it later served as a Federal Reserve Bank.

Federal Hall was built with a deference toward prominent ancient empires and their lessons of history. The Doric columns of the facade stood as a tribute to the Parthenon and Greek democracy. The domed ceiling inside served as a reminder of the Pantheon and the Roman Empire's economic might.

On September 6, 2002, members of the United States Congress gathered at Federal Hall to show support for the city that was still recovering from the terrorists' attack just four blocks away. It was the first meeting by Congress in New York since 1790.

On June 6, 2006, the site would boast yet another first. When George Maxwell stood at the top of the stairs and received the VeriChip, history would record the day that the banking industry truly ushered in a cashless society. Maxwell intentionally chose the site for its historical significance, as well as its proximity to the New York Stock Exchange located diagonally across Wall and Nassau Streets.

The New York Stock Exchange was one of the few remaining holdouts where trading was done entirely on the floor rather than electronically. Maxwell believed that stocks could be easily traded anywhere and that the Wall Street location only served as a prestigious address. Hopefully, the powerful brokerage and banking communities would be watching and would be convinced.

The throng of protestors had almost made its way through the streets to the reserved spot in front of Federal Hall. On the way, Melinda noticed that the wind had picked up but thought it was due to the gusts swirling around the tall buildings that were packed so closely together. She thought the skyscrapers blocked the sun from reaching the street, and that was the reason for the increased darkness. The chants were so loud they drowned out the slow rumble of thunder in the distance.

Once the group had settled in around the platform and Melinda had a chance to focus on her surroundings, she finally noticed the gray clouds overhead that were swirling in an odd counter-clockwise direction. She watched as several of the protestors nervously looked up at the sky and checked their watches. It was 8:45 AM, and the spring storm was approaching faster than predicted. The dignitaries from International Bank of Commerce, One World Bank, and Global Financial Bank would have to hurry this news conference along if they were going to beat the rain.

CHAPTER THIRTY

Throughout the course of world history there have been volcanoes that formed as well as destroyed islands and other land masses of habitation. Earthquakes have swallowed up entire cities, along with their citizens. Tornadoes have ripped across miles of open space, leaving only death and destruction in their paths. Hurricanes and typhoons have been given names and personified in recognition of their power. Invariably, after each dreadful and shocking display of nature, survivors felt either comforted or cursed as they rationalized that the inexplicable was, "An act of God."

God had been blamed for all sorts of calamity and misfortune, and for causing great harm and loss to the helpless inhabitants of this planet. The tsunami that hit South Asia on December 26, 2004, was one of the worst natural disasters in recent memory. More than two hundred fifteen thousand lost their lives; even more still live in refugee camps and rely on handouts to survive.

Some in the region believe that God did, in fact, have His hand in sending the tsunami because it ended a decade old bloody conflict between the Indonesian government and terrorist guerillas in the provincial capital of Banda Aceh. It changed the priorities and focus of the political, as well as, the personal interests. It forced the people to rely on each other for survival. Most of all, the tsunami reminded the people of the world that they were no match of the forces of nature created by the Almighty.

And so, as George Maxwell and his colleagues from Global Financial Bank and the leaders from the other two banks and their entourages planned their arrival at Federal Hall around 9:00 AM, another act of God was forming in the heavens and scheduled to hit lower Manhattan shortly thereafter.

There was no mistaking it now, the severe storm was getting closer. The rolls of thunder were louder and closer together. The sky was so dark that the street lights had come back on. Melinda was at the front of the group, closer to the stage. The protestors had pressed their way in and had pushed to get as close to the platform as possible. She searched the crowd for Richard and her friends so they wouldn't be separated in case they had to make a run for cover. She finally spotted Richard toward the back of the group, but she couldn't get his attention.

It was almost 9:00 AM, and the crowd had grown restless. The chants had become louder and more urgent in competition to be heard over each other. Several protestors played to the news cameras and provided plenty of rhetoric for the evening news clips.

When the procession of black limos and vans finally turned the corner and parked in front of the New York Stock Exchange, the crown erupted into a frenzy. Melinda hadn't noticed previously, but, apparently, the banks had recruited their own cheering section as well. It was quite a sight.

There were civil libertarians chanting and promoting their agenda in support of individual privacy rights. They were joined by protestors who warned that the implanted bank chip was dangerously close to the mark of the Beast. And, to balance it all out, there were proponents of the new technology who denounced the others as either religious zealots or left wing extremists. Placards jumped up and down to the beat of the chanting as the three factions competed to be heard. The news cameras caught it all.

George Maxwell and the others stepped out of their vehicles and hurried toward the platform. He waved to his supporters, who'd been carefully positioned close to the cameras. His assistants quickly organized and seated those on the stage in order to get the announcement and demonstration underway.

Maxwell stepped up to the podium and tested the microphone. He held up both arms with his palms toward the crowd in an attempt to silence it. Slowly, the protestors gave way.

"Thank you. I understand your positions and recognize your right to voice your concerns. All I ask is that you keep it civil and not try to interfere with our presentation. We need to get started. I understand there's a possible storm on the way."

Maxwell welcomed all of the dignitaries and visitors. He followed with the introductions of Global Financial's officers and board of directors in attendance. He recognized the other banks' presidents and their directors. He gave a short recap of the history of Federal Hall and the many "firsts" that had taken place on that very location.

The crowd listened politely, some with genuine interest and without interrupting as Maxwell had requested. Melinda watched for any sign that he might have reservations or that he was wavering with his support and enthusiasm of the event. She saw none.

"And now," George said waving, his arm toward the historic structure behind him, his broad smile beaming, "let's get started with another first at this most appropriate site and on this most appropriate date."

George was caught up in the moment and the thrill that his visionary plan for Global Financial Bank was about to become a reality. He'd forgotten all about any hesitation he'd experienced only a short time ago during the ride to Federal Hall. In front of a captive audience, with the cameras rolling, Maxwell was at his best. He felt like a winner just as he had on so many other occasions, and he spoke with confidence.

"It was just one year ago today that Global Financial Bank experienced the unfortunate loss of some of its customers' personal data. Earlier last year, International Bank of Commerce and One World Bank dealt with similar losses. The boards of these three banks have responded with swift and decisive actions that will help protect their customers against future loss." George waved his hand toward the directors in attendance. They nodded their mutual admiration to Maxwell in response. The supporters of the banks clapped and cheered on cue.

Maxwell continued. "Today marks the beginning of a new world order of banking. Global Financial Bank has been and continues to be a leader for advances in national and international commerce transactions."

It was noticeable to those on the platform that Maxwell had omitted International Bank and One World Bank in his last comment. The directors from those banks adjusted nervously in their chairs and exchanged glances and raised eyebrows of displeasure. The omission had been intentional. Maxwell was willing to share some, but not all of the credit. He hadn't gotten this far in his career by passing up an opportunity to distinguish himself among his competitors. "Folks, what you're about to witness will amaze you."

He motioned for the nurse to step forward. The portable scanner was already positioned on a table to the right of the podium. It drew its power from a temporary electrical line that had been installed earlier that morning.

The cameramen balanced their equipment on their shoulders and adjusted the focus on their lenses. The reporters made some quick scribbles on their notepads. They spoke into their handheld microphones as they looked straight into the camera. The live coverage was rolling.

Melinda watched George smile and beam as he removed his suit coat and began to roll up the cuff on his right arm. She thought of running onto the platform to try to stop him but quickly subdued her emotions after surveying the tight security surrounding the area. Once again the noise from the crowd rose to a deafening crescendo, and the placards jumped to life.

The nurse sterilized a spot on George's right wrist and raised the syringe containing the microchip from the table. Melinda watched with horror. The scene was surreal. She felt paralyzed and suspended in that moment. She no longer heard the noise from the crowd. She became oblivious to those pushing against her and shouting their mantras. She stared straight ahead at her son and silently cried in anguish. *Lord, please don't let this happen!*

Suddenly, the sky lit up, and a blinding bolt of lighting ripped through the clouds. It was immediately followed by a deafening clap of thunder that shook the ground. The startled crowd's chants were replaced by shrieks and screams.

George snapped his head around and looked up at the black threatening clouds spinning overhead. He turned to face the others on the stage and saw the concerned looks on their faces. They were gathering their things and preparing to leave. He looked out over the street and saw that many of the spectators were scrambling to find cover, and that the reporters and cameramen were packing up their equipment. *No, this can't be happening.*

He looked to his right at the nurse who was still holding the syringe but was now uncertain what to do with it. To his left, he looked out over the sparse group still in the street and spotted Melinda in the melee. She wasn't moving. She hadn't left her place at the front of the platform. Instead, she was standing there looking straight at him. Their eyes locked on each other. George had a look of utter despair. She could tell he was stunned.

Another flash immediately followed by an even louder explosion of thunder broke their stare. By now, the platform had emptied, and the guests were headed to the waiting vans and limos. The wind gusts had lifted the greenery out of its containers and thrown it across the steps of Federal Hall.

In the midst of the chaos, one of the news reporters urgently called out, “I’ve just been informed by my producer that we are under a tornado warning. A funnel cloud has been spotted within five miles of here and . . .”

The reporter never had a chance to finish her breaking news report. Just then, another bolt of lightning dropped out of the sky, hit the electric scanner, and sent any remaining spectators and protestors scrambling for shelter and safety.

George Maxwell jumped back to avoid the sparks flying from the scanner, grabbed his suit coat and wrapped it around the nurse. He hurried her to one of the waiting vans. The streets quickly cleared as the storm hit with its full fury, and rain and hail pounded the concrete.

Within seconds, the stage, the chairs, the greenery—the history making event—had been swept away by an Act of God. The only evidence of the event that remained was the deserted podium standing next to the smoldering scanner. As the rain saturated its casing and extinguished the thin ribbon of smoke rising from the metal, all that was left was the putrid smell of scorched electrical wires.

CHAPTER THIRTY-ONE

The rain fell in torrents and quickly flooded the sidewalks and streets. Melinda sloshed through the water as it rushed toward the gutters. She slipped into a portal of one of the buildings adjacent to Federal Hall.

She stood alone and huddled against the concrete waiting for the storm to pass. Her clothes were pasted against her skin. The lightning flashed in rapid succession across the sky, and at times, it was blinding. The sidewalk beneath her feet vibrated with each crash of thunder. The tornado sirens echoed throughout the streets.

Melinda cupped her hands around her eyes for protection as she looked out on the street for any sign of Richard or her friends. It was no use; she couldn't see anything or anyone. The wind was gusting again, and the rain was blowing sideways over the entire area. Surely they had found cover and didn't try to make it back to the car. As soon as the lightning stopped, she'd try to call Richard on her cell phone.

In the midst of the fury of nature, alone in a doorway in the Financial District in lower Manhattan, Melinda Andrews felt peace. She felt safe and was not afraid. She loved storms, especially tornadoes. They had always fascinated her. Usually, when weather reports warned of an approaching tornado, rather than seek shelter, she looked out her windows or stepped outside in hope of seeing it. She was mesmerized by their rotating funnels and the winds that accompanied them.

Wasn't it just like God, not only to answer her prayer to stop the demonstration, but also to do so by sending a tornado? Two blessings in one. Melinda smiled and drew in a sigh of relief. For now at least, George's plans were put on hold. She imagined that he must be very disappointed with the day so far. She wished that she could somehow reach him, talk to him, learn his intentions.

The storm had passed. The rain weakened to a light shower. The black clouds were blowing off to the East. Behind them she could see a hint of blue sky and calm.

The streets were filling again as spectators ventured out to survey the damage. Within minutes, lower Manhattan had returned to business as usual. Melinda stepped out of her shelter and headed in the direction of Global Financial Bank to find George. She pulled her cell phone from her pocket and called Richard to tell him she was safe and to meet her there.

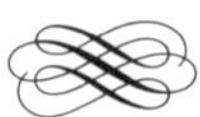

George Maxwell had jumped out of the limo as soon as it pulled up in front of the bank building. He needed to get inside and out of the storm before it got any worse, if that was possible. He rushed through the lobby to his express elevator that ran non-stop to the seventy-fifth floor and his office suite. Maxwell had always kept a fresh change of clothes in his private dressing area. He had to get out of his drenched suit and change his shoes before greeting the public. Image was everything.

On the ride up, he considered the day's events so far. It had not gone as planned, but maybe some things could still be salvaged. Hopefully, the public would still respond to the invitation to attend the champagne reception and open an account with the new technology.

George caught a glimpse of his reflection in the smoke mirrored interior of the elevator. His once perfectly groomed hair and clothing were in total disarray. The suit and silk tie were probably ruined and would likely be discarded. His Italian leather shoes were starting to tighten and rub against his feet. Already the day had cost George several thousands of his own personal funds. He hoped Global Financial would fare better.

Without warning, the elevator abruptly jolted, then dropped, throwing George to the floor. He slammed his head against the marble beneath the chair rail as he landed. He heard the whine of the elevator cables as they slowed to a stop. The ceiling light flickered off and on a couple of times before finally leaving George in total darkness. Within seconds, the back-up power clicked on and provided a welcomed beam of light from a corner of the wall. *Oh, for heaven's sake, what next?*

Maxwell stood up and hit the emergency intercom button on the panel to call for help.

"Is anyone there?" He waited. No response. "Hello, hello, can anyone hear me?" He waited. Nothing. George closed his eyes, drew a deep breath, and let out an exasperated sigh. *Can this day get any worse?*

He tried the emergency button again. "Please, can someone help me?" His hope was only momentarily restored by the voice from the speaker.

"Hello? You still there? Everything's OK. Had a power outage from the storm. Transformer got hit. Regular power'll be back as soon as possible. We're trying to conserve, so just sit tight." Click.

"Wait! Wait! This is George Maxwell. Can't you get me out of this elevator?" There was no response.

George sat down in a corner and leaned back against the wall. He pulled his legs up to his chest, propped his elbows on his knees, and held his head in his hands. He winced as he inadvertently brushed the swollen knot that had already formed on his forehead from the fall a few minutes earlier. George Maxwell was not having a good day.

He sat on the floor in the elevator and realized that there probably wouldn't be at least six hundred new accounts opened by noon that day. If the storm hadn't kept people away, the power outage would. He guessed that the back up generators were supplying the power for the essential functions to secure the building and provide at least minimum service. The express elevator to his presidential office suite wasn't considered a mandatory function to warrant immediate attention. So, even if customers did happen to venture out, he would miss it all if he didn't get out of the elevator

He thought back to the botched news event just a short time ago at Federal Hall . . . the unexpected downpour . . . the scorched portable scanner. *How can such a carefully planned event go down the drain—literally—in seconds?* he wondered.

He recalled seeing Melinda and the look on her face as their eyes met just before they'd all run for cover. He wondered if she'd found shelter in time, if she was safe. He wondered if she was relieved that the storm had interrupted the demonstration, almost before it even began. *What about that?* he thought. *Another coincidence?*

For almost twenty minutes, Maxwell sat with his knees against his chest before the steel cables jolted back to life and the ceiling lights flashed back on. He stood up when the elevator continued its rise to the seventy-fifth floor. He was chilled and stiff from sitting in his wet clothes huddled in the corner. As soon as the doors opened, George bolted out and headed straight for his closet. He had to change and get back downstairs to try to get control of this situation.

CHAPTER THIRTY-TWO

Although George Maxwell tried to remain optimistic as he headed down to the bank lobby and the waiting reception, it didn't last. When he exited the elevator and walked into the lobby, he saw several waiters standing around the room with silver trays full of appetizers, ready to serve. He saw the champagne fountain and sparkling crystal flutes ready for a toast. He saw the bank cashiers who'd been trained to operate the scanner waiting to demonstrate its use. But, other than the bank employees and temporary wait staff, the lobby was empty. Even the legal department and bank officers had returned to their offices on the executive floor of the building to work on other business. There wasn't a single customer in sight.

Maxwell's heart sank. His question in the elevator had been answered. Yes, this day could still get worse. He tried to fake a smile for everyone and pump up their spirits. He didn't want them to get discouraged, and he didn't want them to know of the despair he was feeling as well. They politely nodded and returned his smile, but he hadn't fooled them. Everyone knew how much planning—and money—had gone into this event and how much Mr. Maxwell had looked forward to it.

In unison, everyone's head jerked toward the revolving door as soon as it began to spin. A customer! A very water logged customer! Someone who'd braved the torrential downpour and made it in. The figure had a soggy newspaper draped over its head. The waiters snapped to attention. Maxwell stepped forward with his hand outstretched to welcome their first arrival. The figure lowered the newspaper from around its head, and George Maxwell stared straight at the face of Melinda Andrews. An awkward moment passed between them as she accepted his handshake. He took the newspaper from her and dropped it into the brass trash receptacle by the door.

"Welcome . . . uh, . . . I'm sure you're not here to open one of our a new accounts, but welcome, anyway. I was worried about you. That storm came up so quickly. Not much time for everyone to find cover. Can I get you anything?" he babbled.

"No, I don't want to bother you," she calmly replied. "I just wanted to see if you were all right. The lightning struck so close to you, well . . . I was a little worried. What happened to your head?" she asked as she noticed the bump and bruise that had formed.

George instinctively touched the sore spot on his forehead above his left eye. "I hit it against the wall in the elevator. The power went out and . . . it's a long story. I'm fine. Just one more casualty of the morning."

"So far, this day hasn't gone very well for you, has it?" She sounded genuinely sympathetic. "I know you must be very disappointed." She looked around the lobby.

"Please, at least have a cup of coffee." George tried to divert her attention. "You must be chilled by now. Did you walk over from Federal Hall?"

"Yes, after the rain finally let up. I guess I can stay long enough for a cup of coffee."

George motioned for one of the waiters to bring two coffees and led Melinda to a side office where they could talk privately. "I don't mind telling you, but I don't want them," he said, crooking his head in the direction of the employees, "to know. But, yes, I'm extremely disappointed. I've been planning this day for months. The bank has spent a lot of money to make it special." He offered her a chair and his handkerchief to dry her face.

"George, what did the adoption papers say?" Melinda asked, deliberately changing the subject. The question caught George off guard, but he was able to maintain his composure. He adjusted in his chair before answering. He studied Melinda's face as he carefully chose his words.

"You already know," he confirmed then hesitated before saying, "is that why you're here?"

"I suppose it is." Melinda debated whether she should say anymore. Finally, she continued. "A chance like this, a chance for someone in my shoes, I guess I should say, doesn't come along very often. I'm grateful to God for it. When I relinquished you as a newborn, I never thought I'd see you again." She smiled and searched his eyes for understanding.

George returned the smile and waited for her to finish. She obviously had more to say, and he didn't want to interrupt.

"I'm proud of you, George. You've done well. I wouldn't blame you if you didn't want for us to get to know each other."

She chuckled slightly. "We haven't got off to a very smooth start—on opposite sides already. But, I would like to know you and for you to know me. For you to know my . . . the rest of my family." She struggled to find the right words. Even though she had known George only a few days, she already thought of him as family.

"Where do you see this going?" he inquired.

"That will be up to you. You know my convictions about your plans for Global Financial, and those won't change. Richard and I will continue to oppose this embedded chip. Our friends are committed to speaking out against it, as well. We're pretty well organized now, and we plan to be even more proactive and vocal."

They sat and looked at each other without saying a word. Both were torn between two beliefs, and neither one saw how they could find a compromise. George's whole life was consumed by his career with Global Financial Bank. Melinda hoped he'd walk away from it if it meant he'd have to take or promote the embedded chip.

Melinda finally spoke and broke the silence. "Hey, thanks for the coffee. But really, I've got to go. Richard's supposed to meet me out front. He's probably waiting." She stood up and handed George her cup and saucer. She held on to his handkerchief.

"Sure." George sighed. "It was kind of you to stop by and check on me. I'll think about what you said, I promise. Really, I will," he said sincerely. They started walking toward the front door. About half way there, George reached for her elbow and gently turned her to face him. "Say, just out of curiosity, did you pray for that storm to hit this morning?" he joked, although he was halfway serious.

Melinda smiled. She considered her answer before she spoke. "I believe God is in control of all things. The question is—do you?" She hesitated and cocked her head. "George, have you even thought about today's date?"

"What do you mean?" he asked bewildered.

"It's June 6, 2006, you know, 6-6-6, the number of the Beast. It's chi xi stigma in the original Greek text, if you're interested," she offered.

"Whoa! I hadn't even realized it," he responded with genuine surprise. A somber expression crossed his face. He lowered his voice. "Do you suppose that's another coincidence?"

"That's something else you'll have to decide," Melinda answered and gently patted his arm. "I really must go now. I'll be praying for you, George." She smiled softly and cupped her hand against his face. "You know how to reach me."

George watched her walk out of the lobby and through the revolving door. Maybe he would see her again, but right now—he just didn't know. A lot had happened in the past few days, and he wasn't sure how he felt about all of it. He did know that he still had a bank to run. He'd made a life for himself at Global Financial—a very comfortable life. He was respected by a lot of powerful and influential people. *How does one just walk away from all of that?*

Maxwell willed his attention back to the business of the day. He looked around. It was the same as earlier, not a customer in sight.

CHAPTER THIRTY-THREE

Someone or something had to pump some life back into this day. As George Maxwell walked away from the revolving door, he surveyed the room. He recognized the look of defeat on his employees' faces. Their expressions conveyed their disappointment as they looked around the empty lobby. The waiters shuffled aimlessly, moving from one side of the room to another, attempting to look busy. Occasionally, they'd glance toward the front door and windows for any sign that the anticipated crowd was gathering on the sidewalk before making its grand entrance into the bank lobby.

Maxwell realized that his own body language communicated fatigue and weakness. He straightened his tie, pulled his shoulders back, and quickened his step toward the cashiers.

"From the expression on everyone's faces, you'd think it was the end of the world. Well, it's not! We had a minor setback this morning, but just look outside." He enthusiastically waved toward the large front wall of glass that provided a full view of the sky. "The storm has passed. It's sunny!" George Maxwell sounded like a cheerleader.

A few of the employees' expressions perked up a little in response. They stood straighter and offered a smile to their boss.

"That's more like it," Maxwell said encouragingly. He moved about the room as he spoke, trying to establish eye contact with each one. "Look, I can't explain what's happened to everyone. Maybe they're on their way. Has anyone heard if our directors are still planning to stop by?"

A few shook their heads and shrugged their shoulders. They didn't know. Maxwell hesitated and thought a moment. "What about the nurse? Is she still here?" he asked as he craned his neck to look around at the faces.

"I'm over here," a reluctant voice answered. All heads turned in the direction of a petite young woman who appeared to be in her late twenties. Her wet hair hung lifeless around her face. She'd changed out of her soaking wet uniform into a borrowed oversized sweatshirt and pants belonging to one of the secretaries who regularly used the bank's on-site gym. Maxwell hardly recognized her, but she did look a lot calmer now that bolts of lightning weren't snapping around her.

"Good," Maxwell said. He beamed as he clapped his hands in three quick successions. "Then nothing has changed. We're still going forward with our plans. And to show that I still have complete confidence in this new procedure, I'll be the first customer."

George Maxwell removed his suit coat and handed it to one of the cashiers. He once again rolled up his cuff to expose his right wrist and, still smiling, looked at the nurse for further instructions. When she realized that he was serious, she reached for the supply tray that held several alcohol wipes, some medicated cotton swabs, and the VeriChip syringe.

There was a utility table with several straight back chairs around it that had been set up in the center of the lobby for the occasion. The nurse motioned for Maxwell to follow her. She lowered the supply tray to the table and sat in one of the chairs. Maxwell sat across from her. The others crowded around to watch. The waiters perched their silver trays on their shoulders.

"Mr. Maxwell, this procedure is supposed to be relatively painless, but I can numb the area with a topical cream, if you prefer," the nurse offered.

Maxwell shook his head. "No, that won't be necessary. I don't want it getting out to the press and the public that I had to have an anesthetic before getting chipped," he joked. "And speaking of the press, we'll need to do a news release. Somebody take notes for our public relations department to use to prepare a memo." Maxwell smiled as he spoke in an upbeat manner. He was determined to be optimistic and to demonstrate confidence. Hopefully, his attitude would be contagious.

The nurse opened one of the packets containing a sterile cleansing pad. She rubbed the pad over Maxwell's wrist in a circular motion. He willed himself to watch the whole process. As the nurse held the syringe against the flesh, a camera flashed and captured the moment. At least one cashier had come prepared to record the day. Nervous laughter broke out as someone jokingly referred to the lightning earlier that morning.

There was just a slight sting as the microchip pierced Maxwell's skin. It was probably due more to the alcohol that was still wet his wrist than from the device itself. A few winced ever so slightly, but most let out a sigh of relief and finally allowed a genuine smile to cross their faces. Impromptu applause and cheers rang out as the spectators exchanged excited comments with each other.

"Who's next?" Maxwell challenged as he jumped up and offered his chair. There was hesitation at first, but it quickly gave way to a spirit of comradery among the group. If the bank president was willing to step up and lead by setting the example, the others were willing to follow.

One by one, each employee offered his or her right wrist to the nurse and bravely received the VeriChip—all without any numbing anesthetic. Afterwards the group drank a glass of champagne as George Maxwell offered a toast to their courage and cooperation. He held his crystal flute above his head as he addressed his cohorts.

"To the fine people of Global Financial Bank. You're why this bank is a standard against which all others are measured. I thank you for your loyalty and dedication. Salud!"

"Hear, hear!" they replied as they raised their glasses and then emptied them.

The reception and morning of celebration weren't exactly as Maxwell had envisioned they would be, but everyone made the best of it. And, before noon, Global Financial had six new customers—the nurse and the five waiters.

The day didn't fare much better for International Bank of Commerce or One World Bank. Both had only a minimal number of new accounts using the new technology. No one could say for sure if it was because of the inclement weather or because of the negative publicity that led up to the event. Either way, it apparently would take a little more time before the public warmed up to the idea of having a computer chip embedded in their flesh.

For the next two weeks, it was business as usual for George Maxwell, nothing out of the ordinary. June 6th had come and gone much like any other day. In the days that followed, he hoped he wasn't being paranoid, but it felt as if some of his colleagues were avoiding him. He noticed that they weren't as solicitous of his opinion. They didn't laugh at his jokes as loudly as before. They lowered their heads and pretended to be preoccupied with work when he walked by their offices. Even Elizabeth Hume was more distant.

"Helen, what's going on with everyone?" he finally asked his secretary one morning.

"Excuse me, sir? I'm not certain what you mean."

"Haven't you noticed?"

"Noticed what, Mr. Maxwell?"

"The mood in the air, the look on people's faces. Everyone seems to be so busy . . . so preoccupied with work . . . less talkative. Haven't you noticed?"

"Not really, sir. Maybe they're still trying to catch up with all of the work that got pushed aside while we were preparing for June 6th," Helen offered, trying to appease him.

"Um, I hadn't thought of that. You could be right," Maxwell replied, pretending to accept her explanation. He let Helen think he believed her, but he wasn't convinced at all. He was sure that he wasn't imagining things. Something was different. Something didn't feel right.

In an effort to generate some publicity for Global Financial Bank, Maxwell made sure that the public relations department sent an announcement and the cashier's snapshot of him receiving the VeriChip to several newspapers and business journals with large circulations. One journal, *World Finance Monthly*, printed a story about the event in its July issue in a section about banking trends. The photo turned out to be a complimentary close up of Maxwell smiling as he held out his wrist for the nurse. But, the accompanying article, filled with editorial comments, was highly critical of the bungled event and Global Financial. Why hadn't there been a back-up plan to hold the demonstration indoors? Why wasn't the press invited to Global Financial Headquarters for the reception? Why hadn't the bank countered the initial bad press and opposition with some positive news releases about the success of the chip to date?

Vivo Solana still carried his subscription to the *World Finance Monthly*. From the terrace overlooking the ocean at his secluded summer home in the Hamptons, Solana carefully read the article in the July issue and studied the photo of George Maxwell. He lowered the magazine and stared out over the water for several minutes as he thought back to his days at Global Financial. Once again, he felt the twinge of hurt and disappointment that he'd experienced the day he left—or the day he was forced out—if he wanted to maintain any self respect at all. He regained his focus and looked back at Maxwell's face in the photo and glared with contempt. *How does it feel, George?*

CHAPTER THIRTY-FOUR

Switzerland had long been regarded a safe haven for money. Swiss banks held thirty-five per cent of the world's private and corporate funds with an estimated value of more than three trillion Swiss francs (CHF).

Politically, the country was run with an efficient, but strictly limited government. Historically, the right to privacy in one's financial affairs had been a tenet of Swiss law. Thus, Swiss banking laws were unique and appealed to those for whom secrecy was valued.

In the 1930s, during Nazi Germany, there were no privacy measures in place, and the names on bank accounts were readily ascertainable. German citizens were executed for holding a Swiss bank account. Afterward, to protect the identity of the owner, Swiss banks offered accounts to individuals and corporations using only a numbered account. Names were not used anywhere on the bank statements and were not revealed to anyone unless authorized by the owner.

The landmark Swiss Banking Law of 1934 codified this banking courtesy into law. The law recognized that the right to privacy belonged to the customer, not the bank. As a result, it became a criminal offense, subject to imprisonment, for a banker to divulge information about a customer. Swiss bank employees were required to sign a confidential agreement as a condition of employment.

Foreigners who shared the same philosophy about banking secrecy had found Swiss banks among the safest in the world. To open an account, a person needed only to verify his or her identity, the source of the deposits, and the owner's place of residence.

Switzerland wasn't the only European country that prized secrecy. Luxembourg and Liechtenstein also allowed numbered accounts. The Cook Islands, the Caribbean, the Bahamas, and the Cayman Islands were also popular offshore banking destinations that guarded the privacy of the customer. However, the Swiss had hundreds of years of political stability—the last war in which they fought was in the 15th century—and the Swiss had well-educated bankers, fluent in many languages.

And so it was that Vivo Solana choose Geneva, Switzerland as his safe haven. He'd done his homework about international banking laws, and the Swiss laws appeared to be the most attractive to meet his needs.

The time was right, and Vivo Solana knew it. He'd read all of the letters to the editor protesting the VeriChip leading up to June 6th. He'd read about the severe storm that had struck and the resulting chaos on the steps of Federal Hall that morning. He'd read about the poor turn out the three banks had so far in response to the new technology. He could only imagine the heat that the three presidents must be taking from their boards of directors. He guessed that The Big Three, and especially George Maxwell, were scratching their heads about now, wondering what had gone wrong. Yes. The time was right.

George Maxwell had failed to deliver on his promise to revolutionize the banking industry. Solana knew that Maxwell had to be feeling less confident in his ability to predict the future for Global Financial. That would make him more vulnerable. It was time for Solana to cash in on his scheme that had been on hold, waiting for the right opportunity to maximize the results. It was time for Vivo Solana to contact his fellow crook, Raul Vachon.

Solana had met Raul Vachon a few years earlier through a discreet contact in the underworld. Vachon had provided the necessary introduction and personal recommendation for Solana to set up his own secret bank account with a private banker in Switzerland. Later on, Vachon had proved to be a reliable assistant when Vivo needed help finding a secure place to deposit money until it was clean enough to use. Now, Vivo Solana needed Vachon's services once again.

"Hello, my friend," Solana greeted his co-conspirator. They never addressed each other by name except in private. "You recall the business transaction that we discussed a few months ago?"

"Ah, of course, amigo. Is that the reason you are calling?"

"It is. Have you kept up with the recent events surrounding our, shall we say 'client?'"

"I have," Vachon answered with a chuckle. "I would imagine that the leadership could be somewhat distracted, maybe vulnerable after such a fiasco."

"Exactly. Good minds think alike. It's time. Let's move in—hit them while they're down."

"Are you sure you can still access the appropriate data?" Vachon asked cautiously.

"Absolutely!" Solana snapped with confidence. "Nothing has changed. I can handle it from here. You make the arrangements on your end."

"Of course," Vachon eagerly replied. "Consider it done."

"We'll need at least thirteen separate accounts," Solana instructed. "Unless you think you should distribute our clients' assets even more. I will rely on your judgment."

"My friend, you know I have no clients, only serial numbers." Vachon laughed at his cleverness. "I will get back with you soon with all of the details."

Raul Vachon had mentored Vivo Solana for the past few years and helped him amass a personal fortune. Raul Vachon had several personal bankers available to help him set up secret bank accounts. Some of his highly sensitive accounts were referenced by serial codes that referenced other serial codes that were buried in yet even more codes known only to a few. These accounts were used to create a false history for unlaundered funds from various corrupt governments, illicit arms sales, or drug trafficking. After time, and several transactions on the books, the cash achieved the appearance of legitimacy and was ready to enjoy.

Solana had always been satisfied with the results and never questioned how the channeled funds got into the secret accounts and back out again. Don't ask. Don't tell. That was the working arrangement between the two men. Solana supplied the assets, Vachon safeguarded them in total secrecy. No one other than the few involved ever knew the details. And, each of the players received a healthy reward for his discretion. Once the assets arrived in Geneva, they were guarded by the banking privacy laws and were nondiscoverable. It was just business.

It was time for Vivo Solana to make good on the promise he'd made himself after he left Global Financial. He'd been patient, but now the time was right.

CHAPTER THIRTY-FIVE

Monday mornings were always busy for George Maxwell and for Global Financial, after being closed for the weekend. Maxwell usually enjoyed the return to work and plunging into the new week with all of the challenges it brought. As a general rule, there were more transactions, more activity in the global markets, and more phone calls on Monday mornings than on any other day of the week.

Throughout his tenure as president of Global Financial, George Maxwell had made a point to contact the bank's directors personally on a regular basis. He traditionally spoke to at least two or three of them at the start of his day on Monday mornings. Maxwell had always initiated the calls. It was his way to show respect for their position and contribution as a director, but mostly, he enjoyed discussing current events and maintaining contact with his board members. So, on this particular Monday morning, he was surprised to see the stack of messages for him to call five of the directors the minute he got to the office.

What's going on? he wondered. *Surely, I haven't forgotten about a conference call,* he thought. He quickly perused the daily itinerary that Helen had placed on his desk along with the phone messages. He pushed his intercom button. "Helen, did you personally take these phone messages from these directors?"

"Yes, sir."

"Did they say why they were calling?"

"No, sir, just that you needed to call them the minute you got in."

"OK, thanks." His voice trailed off. He looked at the stack of messages again. Randall Dixon's was on the top.

"Helen, you still there?"

"Yes, Mr. Maxwell."

"I need you to get Mr. Dixon on the phone for me."

"Certainly, sir."

Maxwell removed his suit jacket and hung it on the valet next to the credenza behind his desk. He sat at his desk with his arms folded across his chest and waited for Helen to page him. He had that feeling again that something was wrong. Why would five directors call him unexpectedly the first thing Monday morning and insist that he call them back with such urgency? What was so important that it couldn't wait? Maxwell jumped at the beep of the intercom. "Mr. Dixon is holding on your private line, sir."

"Thank you, Helen." Maxwell hit the button to connect the call.

"Good morning, Randall. How are you?" Maxwell asked enthusiastically.

"Not good," Randall Dixon thundered. Even in his anger, he still managed to pronounce "good," as if it had two syllables. "Have you spoken to any other directors yet?

"No. About what?" Maxwell answered bewildered. His mind raced as he tried to reason what could have Dixon so upset.

"Our accounts, our holdings," Dixon bellowed. "Haven't you heard?"

"Take it easy, Randall. Slow down. What are you talking about? Whose accounts?"

"We've been stripped. Somebody got into our accounts, all of them," he yelled. "Stripped them by way of electronic transfer!" Randall Dixon was near hysteria as he spoke. He was worth millions, or at least he had been, and he loved his money.

George Maxwell became dizzy as his mind tried to process what Randall Dixon was saying. He couldn't believe his ears. He fumbled to find the right words.

"Randall, who are you talking about? Whose accounts have been stripped?"

"The bank's directors. Who else would I be talking about?" he said, obviously sneering.

"Randall, that can't happen. There has to be some mistake." Maxwell tried to reassure him. "Those accounts are secure. You have to have the password and other personal information even to access them. No one has that information except the owner and a handful of people who manage the funds. Three, maybe four people at the most. Even then, there are encrypted access codes . . ."

"George, listen to me!" Dixon interrupted. Maxwell could hear him pounding his fist. "You think I'd make this up? Don't tell me it can't happen. Try telling that to the thousands of other customers who lost their assets last year." The sarcasm in his voice was obvious.

"Randall, please, calm down," Maxwell urged. "You're going to give yourself a heart attack. Let me check into this and get back with you. There's got to be a legitimate explanation."

"Well, you better get on it. And don't tell me to calm down. I've heard from seven other directors already this morning. It looks like we've all been hit. There had better be a darn good explanation, and I want to hear it. Today!"

Maxwell hung up the phone. He was stunned. There had to be some mistake he reasoned. But, Randall Dixon and the other directors wouldn't make up something like this. What if everything Dixon had just said was true? How did the thief get into all of their secured accounts?

Maxwell couldn't process all of the questions that were firing through his brain. He fought the anxiety that was pressing in and trying to overwhelm him. He recalled the anguish he'd felt a year ago after he learned of the heist of the computer tapes. *Who is targeting Global Financial and why?* George swallowed hard. He felt panic sweep over him. He could barely breathe.

CHAPTER THIRTY-SIX

Although Maxwell had assured Randall Dixon that there had to be a mistake, that there was a legitimate explanation, that the directors' fortunes were in fact secure, he soon learned otherwise. He also learned that he, too, had been a target. All thirteen of them had been victims of identity theft.

It was obviously the job of an insider. The question now was *who?* There were no clues, no paper trails, no loose ends. It had been a clean heist. The only evidence was that someone had been able to access all thirteen portfolios, even though they were protected by personal security passwords. Someone had been able to authorize the transfer of all thirteen portfolios to a newly established account—or accounts—somewhere out of the country. And, at least for the present time, the transactions were untraceable.

The money, the securities, the bonds, the investments, the wealth—it was all gone. Vanished. All thirteen men were—at least on paper, and for the time being—flat broke. And George

Maxwell could not provide a legitimate explanation. In fact, the more he tried to suggest a cause or explore a motive, the more suspicious the other men became of him. Days passed without any answers. It was becoming impossible for Maxwell to allay their anger and mistrust toward him. Their patience had expired. The more time that passed without any news, and especially without any sign of their missing fortunes, the more restless they all became.

It may have been their need for immediate redress, or their need to find an answer, or their need to blame someone—someone had to be blamed—but it was obvious that the twelve directors were turning against George Maxwell and demanding accountability.

After a week without any real progress or leads on the missing funds, and after a week of lost earnings on their investments, the board of directors called an emergency meeting. The members flew into New York City from all over the country. This time, under these circumstances, they weren't as happy to see each other, and no one was happy to see George Maxwell.

In the space of one hour, by colleagues that he'd once admired and respected, but more importantly, who'd once admired and respected him, George Maxwell was brought low. They accused him of criminal acts and carelessness, and they criticized him of poor leadership. His accusers were wealthy men who'd suddenly and unwittingly been separated from their fortunes. Respect and admiration went by the wayside. Even Doyle Jackson who'd previously been one of his closest allies on the board, spoke to him with utter disgust and looked upon him with scorn.

"George, I supported you and helped you promote that whole VeriChip program to these men. This is how you repay me?" he shouted.

"Doyle, surely you can't believe I had anything to do with the disappearance of these accounts." Maxwell was astonished. "I'm a victim as much as you are," he reminded Doyle.

"C'mon, George," Doyle barked. "Who else would have had complete access to all of our personal information? Of all of us, only you are authorized to use the wire transfer terminal. You could have made it look like you've been stripped also just to avoid suspicion."

The bank's security systems allowed a wire transfer only by an authorized employee and only from a computer with a modem that dialed directly into the network. The computer that stored the most sensitive personal data for all accounts in excess of five hundred thousand dollars was located in a vault-like room behind the highest level of security. Access was gained only after a fingerprint from the right index finger was validated by a reader.

Once inside the computer data bank, a personal identification number was needed in order to authorize a wire transfer. Even then, the transfer couldn't occur without a secondary authorization. If anyone attempted to initiate a transfer without a validated PIN, the PIN was automatically disabled. Generally, passwords were changed every thirty days as another safeguard for legitimate wire transfers.

Maxwell tried to reason with his accusers. "Gentlemen, you've made some very harsh statements against me. I must say, I'm astounded. I assure you we'll get to the bottom of this. But you must be patient. We have to stick together on this."

Although Maxwell tried to convince his board members to stand behind him, they wouldn't be swayed. Someone had to bear the blame. It was obvious that they had come to the meeting with their opinion already formed against him.

And not just for this, but for the utter failure of the VeriChip—the new technology that was supposed to enhance security and attract new customers. Forget that all of them had ratified and voted unanimously to adopt Maxwell's proposal. They never would have been so careless if Maxwell hadn't been so persuasive that the plan was good for Global Financial Bank. The shareholders would demand accountability for their actions and for all of the money that was spent to get the new system up and running.

"I'm telling you, gentlemen," Maxwell urged, "the VeriChip is the future of banking, the future of all commercial transactions. Maybe Global Financial is a little early, maybe the technology needs more time to catch on. But it will, I assure you. There are pilot programs using the technology showing up on college campuses, at convenience stores, fast food drive-ins."

"Mr. Maxwell!" a voice harshly interrupted. The speaker didn't wait to be recognized by the chair before continuing. "Global Financial Bank did not gain its reputation by being careless or trying to be ahead of its time. Global Financial has reached the pinnacle of success by being reliable and trustworthy, good stewards of our customers' money. Recently, the bank has been in the news and sharply criticized by privacy advocates and conservative Christians. I, for one, don't feel comfortable with that. It's not something the founders would have wanted."

As Randall Dixon listened, he sensed the discord against Maxwell that was building. He wanted to distance himself from the support he'd shown Maxwell and the VeriChip at the annual board meeting last fall. Carefully, he formulated a plan that he would suggest to the board when the opportunity presented itself. He found his opening when Doyle Jackson called for action.

"Look, gentlemen, we may all have our own ideas of what happened, but so far, there's no proof. However, we must take control of this situation and make some adjustments in the way we protect our customers' assets, including our own."

Randall Dixon broke in. "You're right, Mr. Jackson. I have given considerable thought to this, and I would like to offer a suggestion."

"Go ahead." Jackson yielded to Dixon. All rules of procedure and protocol had been waived by now. It was obvious that certain individual directors, and not Maxwell, were now running the meeting and on their own terms. They spoke at will without any recognition from the chairman of the board. In fact, most of them didn't even acknowledge that George Maxwell was still present, and they certainly didn't acknowledge that Maxwell was in charge of the agenda.

"Thank you, Doyle," Randall Dixon said. "I believe it is imperative that we proceed with caution. No one really knows who," [he darted his eyes toward Maxwell], "or what is behind this most recent theft, or if it is anyway connected to the one last year. But one thing that's obvious to me is, it's an inside job."

Dixon turned and looked straight at George Maxwell before continuing. He hesitated so that the others in the room could follow his stare. Then, to the complete shock and dismay of George Maxwell, Randall Dixon offered his solution.

"Gentlemen, I believe it's the right thing to do, the prudent thing for all concerned that we ask George Maxwell to step down as president and CEO, at least temporarily, until we get some answers." Dixon tried to soften the impact of his insinuation by smiling and speaking with all of the southern charm he could muster. "Why, . . . it'll appear like the fox guarding the hen house for George to remain while the investigation is going on." Dixon paused and smiled broadly. "Boys, it just doesn't look right."

Maxwell looked around the room as the men continued to discuss his immediate future as if he weren't present. It was the most surreal scene he'd ever witnessed. After a few minutes, all of their words seemed to be spoken in slow motion, and at times, their voices were indistinguishable from one another.

George Maxwell understood the world of finance. He understood how to capitalize on his talents. He understood how to rise to the top and to manipulate people without their knowing it in order to achieve his goals. But, most of all, he understood power. He respected it. He had craved it. He'd earned it. And now he had the eerie feeling that it was slipping away from him. Being George E. Maxwell, President, CEO, and Chairman of the Board of Global Financial Bank—was it really coming to an end?

Maxwell thought back over the last few months and realized he'd become less and less powerful. His plan to lead Global Financial Bank into a new era of banking had failed. His plan to provide better security for Global's customers had failed. His plan to increase the customer base had failed.

Of course the board would suggest that he step down. He should have seen it coming. Someone had to be held accountable for the failed decision to implement the VeriChip and the financial embarrassment it had caused Global Financial. Someone had to be held accountable for the theft of the board members' assets. Even though the assets were insured, and all of the directors' funds would be replaced, someone had to step up and take the blame. George Maxwell would have to be that person. It was just as Randall Dixon had reminded them all: it was the right thing to do.

By a vote of eleven to one Maxwell was placed on administrative leave and stripped of all of his power and titles—indefinitely. Mr. David Cooper was the lone dissenter of the group. As head of a world manufacturer of health care products, he knew full well the immeasurable benefits of the VeriChip. He knew Maxwell was a man of vision and had tried to usher in the state of the art technology for Global Financial. But most of all he knew that George Maxwell was a man of integrity. Unless there was an eye witness and George Maxwell gave a signed confession to the crime, David Cooper would never believe that he had anything to do with the disappearance and apparent theft of the board members' holdings. David Cooper wanted no part of the character assassination of George Maxwell.

Cooper left the building immediately after the vote. He wasn't present to witness the security guard accompany Maxwell to his office to gather up some of his personal items and escort him out of the building.

CHAPTER THIRTY-SEVEN

George Maxwell walked around his office and looked at all of his custom furnishings, his vast collection of books, his valuable sculptures, all of his "stuff." He wondered what people said about him? That he was well read? Liked nice things? Had expensive tastes?

What's happening to me? he wondered. *How can everything spin so vastly out of control—my control—in such a short period of time?* Maxwell looked at his neatly organized, custom-made desk. He loved that desk. He loved this room. He loved this bank. He loved the pressure of his job and the thrill of each new day working at Global Financial.

The emergency board meeting had lasted into the noon hour, so everyone was out for lunch when it adjourned, except Helen. She'd been with Maxwell for many years and was familiar with the board of directors and their ordinary method of conducting business. She could tell that this morning was out of the ordinary.

She'd read the grim expressions on all of the men's faces as they had arrived for the meeting. She had overheard some of the muffled discussion among several of the directors when they caucused before the meeting began. From the tone of their voices and some of their words, Helen could tell that her boss had fallen out of favor. She stayed behind when the other secretaries left for lunch. Her boss might need her.

Helen walked past the guard stationed just outside Maxwell's office and stood in the doorway. She watched as George surveyed the room with his back to her. Finally, she spoke.

"Mr. Maxwell," she said, almost in a whisper.

Maxwell turned around to face her but didn't answer.

"Is there anything I can do for you?" her tone was still hushed.

"That's very kind of you, Helen, but right now, I hardly know what to do myself." Maxwell invited her to come in. "I guess you heard?"

Helen gave a short nod and forced a tight smile. "I'm sorry Mr. Maxwell. I know you never could have done what they're saying. I know you'll be cleared of any wrongdoing, sir."

"Thank you, Helen. But, even so, I know that I'm through here. It never would be the same," Maxwell's voice trailed off. After an awkward moment of silence, Helen spoke.

"I'll make sure that your things are properly packed." She surveyed all of his personal belongings displayed around his office. "I'll supervise it myself, sir." Helen smiled again and timidly walked toward her boss. She extended her right hand. Maxwell took three exaggerated steps and held out his hand to meet hers. Without thinking of office protocol, George pulled Helen toward him with his left hand on her opposite shoulder. They gently hugged each other and fought back their emotions.

Afterward, Helen turned and hurriedly walked out the door. She passed the security guard and her desk and headed down the hallway to the ladies' rest room. Once inside, she leaned against the door and burst into tears.

Throughout the years, she'd been a mother hen to George Maxwell. Jealously she had guarded his calendar and had screened his calls so that every day was as productive for him as possible. It wasn't often that Maxwell forgot a date or an appointment. But if he did, Helen was there to remind him and brief him on the details and make him look good. He was always quick to express his gratitude to her and was generous in sharing the credit for a job well done. Helen had worked for others who were less agreeable. She appreciated Maxwell's kindness and good nature. She would miss him tremendously.

For only a minute more, George stood alone in his office and considered his plight. He realized that he had absolutely no one he could call and talk to about this. Elizabeth Hume couldn't advise him. She would be looking out for the interests of Global Financial and its board of directors. It seemed impossible that they were now on opposite sides of each other.

He couldn't talk to any of the other bank officers. They'd soon be eyeing him with great suspicion as soon as word got out about his "administrative leave." He didn't have any close friends in whom he could confide. And, right now, he didn't trust anyone, so the less said, the better.

"Mr. Maxwell, time to go." The stern voice startled him. He swung around and faced the security guard now standing in the doorway.

"You don't need to worry, I'm not going to take anything that doesn't belong to me, and I know my way out," Maxwell answered, not even trying to mask his sarcasm and rising anger.

"Sorry, sir, but the others will be back from lunch soon, and you'll need to leave before then."

"Oh, of course. We certainly don't want to create a scene. It wouldn't look good for the president to be led off the premises by a security guard, now would it?"

"Sir, I'm just thinking of you." The guard's tone had softened. "The less publicity, the better. Word of this will get out soon enough. I'm trying to help you avoid as much as possible today. If we hurry, we can still beat a lot of questions or at least a lot of stares."

Maxwell realized that the security guard was sincere and trying to help. He nodded to show his appreciation and quickened his step to gather his briefcase and a few of his personal belongings.

Maxwell and the guard rode silently in the express elevator to the lobby. On the way down George wondered if it would be the last time he'd have access to the express elevator that opened directly into his presidential office suite. He could feel his stomach tighten and a lump form in his throat.

The two men stepped out of the elevator, turned toward the lobby, and walked in synchronized steps to the street. Outside, Maxwell looked around for Reese and the waiting limousine, but neither one was in sight.

"Taxi!" the guard called out. George closed his eyes and drew in a deep breath. *Of course there's no limo, no Reese,* he realized. The yellow cab pulled up to the curb, and the guard reached out to open the rear door. Maxwell stepped forward and began lowering himself into the back seat.

"I'm real sorry, sir," the guard offered.

Maxwell halted. His body was bent and suspended between the sidewalk and the inside of the cab. He turned his head and looked back at the guard. "Why the security escort? You know me. You know I wouldn't have caused any trouble."

"I'm just following orders. I don't know anything, sir," the guard answered sincerely. He was cautious with his response. He didn't want to end up on anyone's witness list.

Maxwell slid across the seat, closed the door behind him, and gave the driver his address. The taxi pulled away and headed North toward Carnegie Hill. It was only half past noon—the middle of the work day. George Maxwell had never left the office early a day in his life.

CHAPTER THIRTY-EIGHT

It had been a week since George Maxwell had left his office suite on the seventy-fifth floor of Global Financial Bank's headquarters with a prestigious Wall Street address in lower Manhattan. Maxwell spent his days reading or visiting museums and tourist attractions that he'd never taken the time to enjoy since moving to New York City. He kept a daily journal to record his thoughts and feelings and recollections about anything that might serve as a clue to help solve the crime.

There hadn't been one single phone call from anyone at Global Financial. In fact, there hadn't been a single call from anyone. Maxwell spent his days alone and spoke to no one.

The boxes with his books and collectibles were delivered three days after his departure. He had the movers stack them in the empty spare bedroom. They took up most of the space and stood as a constant reminder of his predicament. He sometimes wondered if anything had taken their place yet on the shelves—his custom made bookshelves—back at Global Financial Bank.

It was the first time ever that George Maxwell had more time on his hands than he could fill. He knew there would come a day when he'd tire of the museums and the parks and the monuments. Then what? What was he supposed to do all day? All week? How long before he could get back to work?

Maxwell was determined to stay positive and hopeful. He tried not to think about the hurt and disappointment he felt. He tried not to become bitter toward the board members who'd turned their backs on him. Still, some days were harder than others. If only he had someone to talk to.

George sat up in bed with a start. Was that the phone or was he dreaming? No! There it rang again. He threw back the covers and swung his legs around and dropped his feet to the floor. He didn't even take time to grab his robe or slide his feet into his house shoes. Instead, George headed down the hallway to the den and picked up the receiver on the third ring. Only a select few had his private unlisted phone number. It must be someone he knew.

"Hello," he answered with a sense of expectancy and short of breath.

"Uh, hello, Mr. Maxwell. I hope I'm not interrupting anything." The voice was familiar, but George couldn't place it at first.

"No, not at all." Maxwell waited for the caller to identify himself and continue.

"Mr. Maxwell, this is Scott Spencer."

That's it. I knew I recognized that voice.

"I'm really sorry, sir, about everything. We're not supposed to discuss it, but I wanted you to know how I felt."

"Thank you, Scott. I appreciate the call. I won't mention it to anyone." It wouldn't be too difficult to keep it a secret. George didn't talk to anyone, but he didn't let on to Scott. "It was considerate of you to call, Scott. I really appreciate it." Just as George was about to hang up the phone, Scott spoke again.

"Uh, wait, sir," he said abruptly. "That's not the only reason I called."

"Oh, excuse me, Scott. I thought you were finished," Maxwell apologized.

"Well . . . you remember Mr. and Mrs. Andrews? We had lunch with them at St. Maggie's Café a few months ago." Maxwell's ears perked up. Of course he remembered.

"Yes, what about them?"

"Well . . . you recall that I'm seeing their daughter, Sarah?"

"Yes." *Where is this going?*

"Well, uh . . . Mrs. Andrews wanted me to see how you're doing. She'd like to hear from you." There, he'd finally got it out. Once again, Scott Spencer had been put in an awkward position between Sarah's folks and Mr. Maxwell. At least this time he didn't have to worry about upsetting his boss.

"Thank you, Scott, for letting me know. Do you have her address? Maybe I'll drop her a line," George said half-heartedly. He took down the street name and number and the Andrews' phone number, and after a little more small talk, they ended their phone call. The two men really didn't have much else to say to each other. George purposely didn't ask Scott anything about Global Financial Bank or the investigation. He didn't want it getting around that he was trying to use a junior associate to glean information about his former colleagues.

The phone call from Scott stayed with George for the rest of the day. He was certain that Melinda Andrews must have heard about his misfortune, and that was the reason she was trying to reach out to him. He tried to imagine what she would say to him and how he'd respond. The last time they'd spoken, several weeks ago, she said she'd be praying for him. That was right after the event at Federal Hall that was supposed to be the kick off to the new technology but instead, turned out to be a disaster. From there, things only got worse. *I wonder what she's been praying?*

Days went by, and then another week. Still no word from anyone. Still no word from Global Financial about the investigation. Still no word about George Maxwell's future. His life was in complete limbo while waiting. Until he was cleared of any wrongdoing, he was too hot for any corporation even to consider hiring. He no longer had control over his career or his future, and they were his life.

George spent his days and nights in complete solitude. He rarely went out even to enjoy the wonderful cuisines in the popular restaurants in Carnegie Hill. Instead, he mostly prepared simple meals and read at the table while he dined alone. His luxurious penthouse in the middle of a neighborhood of wealth and opulence was a lonely place. He may as well be alone on a deserted island as a castaway.

For the first time for as long as George could remember, he needed a friend. More importantly, he wanted a friend.

CHAPTER THIRTY-NINE

After Melinda Andrews left Global Financial Bank's headquarters that morning in June, she wasn't sure if she'd ever see George Maxwell again. She could tell he was unwilling to commit to a friendship, much less, a familial relationship. Even so, she held on to the hope that their reunion wasn't a coincidence, but an act of God. She kept George's handkerchief in her Bible and held it each night as she prayed for God to touch his life.

Melinda had read about the problems at Global Financial Bank and the ongoing investigation. She was shocked that George had been put on administrative leave. Melinda waited and hoped that George would call.

A mother's love for her child never dies. It never stops believing. It never gives up. A mother's love for all her children encourages them in any circumstance, gives them hope in adversity, builds them up to do their best. Next to God's love, it's the purest love there is. When George didn't call, Melinda knew she must try to reach out to him.

She'd prayed before asking Scott to contact George and relay the message for her. She knew he might not want to get involved. Even so, it was the only way for Melinda to reach George, and she was grateful when Scott agreed to make the phone call. But that had been at least two weeks ago, and still she'd heard nothing. *God, why did you bring us together? There has to be something more to this.*

With everyday that passed, Melinda felt more sorrow trying to set in. Some days, the heaviness almost overcame her. Richard tried to console her and encouraged her not to lose hope. As the days passed, one after another, without hearing a word from George, she clung to her belief that God was faithful.

Melinda's hopes and prayers were answered the day the phone call finally came. It was on a Friday morning in early August. George Maxwell had been restless and awake most of the night before. The disconcerting dreams had returned. He couldn't find his way on a deserted road. He hadn't fulfilled a high school graduation requirement. What did these recurring dreams mean? Why wouldn't they leave him alone?

In the early morning hours, George thought about his childhood. He realized that he'd abandoned the lessons of his youth and was no longer the person his parents had reared. He realized that he'd tried to do it all on his own. That he'd set his own course without any regard for God's will for his life. He had become so impressed, so enthralled with his talents and gifts that he'd failed to acknowledge the source of them.

His parents had taught him better, and he'd promised them he wouldn't forget their Godly counsel. But he had.

He was reminded of a Scripture verse that he'd heard his father say whenever George got *too big for his breeches*. "Son, pride goeth before destruction, and an haughty spirit before a fall." George didn't fully understand his father's warning of long ago until now. And now, George Maxwell realized he'd been brought low. His father had been right.

In the early morning hours, George Maxwell fell on his face and cried out to God. He hoped it wasn't too late.

"Hello," Melinda answered. Her heart skipped a beat at the voice on the other end.

"Good morning, Melinda," George replied. He sounded tired and defeated. "I hope I'm not disturbing you."

"Of course not," she said gently. "It's good to hear your voice, George." In fact, she was ecstatic.

"Scott called a few weeks ago and told me you'd asked him to contact me."

"Yes, I wanted to know how you've been doing." There was a pause and then a long sigh.

"Not so good," George finally confessed. "It's been hard being accused of the things that are being said about me. They're pretty serious charges. I never thought I'd been in a situation like this."

For a while, they talked about what had happened, and George tried to explain some of the details. It was good to visit with someone finally and not have to worry about saying the wrong thing. Perhaps she was the only person he knew he could trust completely. During a pause in their conversation George gathered his courage to bring up the real reason for his call.

"I've been thinking about our last conversation—in the bank lobby—you remember?"

"Oh, yes, I've thought a lot about it myself." George was quiet, so Melinda continued. "I still feel the same way as I did then. I still would really like for us to know each other. I can't tell you how thrilled I am to hear from you."

"Well," George said, hesitating and letting out another sigh. "Can I come to see you?"

"Of course! I would love that."

"Can I come today?"

Melinda fought back tears as she and George made plans to meet at her house later that afternoon. She hung up the phone and worshipped God for answering her prayer.

CHAPTER FORTY

George Maxwell didn't own a car. There had been no need for one when Reese and the limousine were at his beck and call. He hadn't used the subway or train in years and was totally unfamiliar with their routes and times of service. He wondered what it would cost to take a cab from Carnegie Hill to New Rochelle. *What does it matter? What else can you do?*

Melinda stood by the front door and watched out the side windows for any sign of George's arrival. After the phone call with George that morning, Melinda baked fresh blueberry muffins. Their aroma filled the air. They were waiting on the kitchen table with a fresh pot of coffee. He was supposed to be there at anytime.

Melinda spotted the yellow taxi as it came down the street and approached her driveway. She opened the front door and stepped outside on the front porch to greet her guest. George waved from the back seat as the car turned in and rolled to a stop. She eagerly watched as he reached over the back seat to pay the driver. He smiled awkwardly at Melinda as he got out of the cab.

She noticed how tired he looked. His face was drawn and gaunt. He was thinner than the last time she'd seen him. Her heart ached as she tried to imagine what he'd gone through the past few weeks. Still, it was an answered prayer that he was there at all. After George's phone call, Melinda and Richard agreed that she should meet with George alone. They hoped he'd feel more comfortable and speak more freely.

As George walked toward her, he extended his right hand. Melinda glanced down at it for only a split second. Then without even thinking, she stepped forward and wrapped her arms around George and embraced him with a mother's love. Melinda thought of the last time she'd held him. He'd been a newborn. He weighed eight pounds and was twenty-one inches long. His whole body had fit along the inside of one of her arms. Now, she had to stand on her tip toes and stretch both arms to reach around him. She cradled her head on his shoulder and gently sobbed.

George tried to hold back his own emotions but finally gave in and let the tears roll down his face unashamed. In that moment he realized that all of the events of the past year had led to this one moment. There had been a purpose behind it after all. He and Melinda had found each other in a way that only the Almighty could have arranged. If George hadn't pushed for Global Financial Bank to implement the use of the VeriChip, their paths might have never crossed.

He realized that his departure from Global Financial and the circumstances that surrounded it had forced him to examine his own life. If he had remained at the bank, he would have continued in his own conceit and never would have realized his need for God. He never would have allowed himself to reach out to anyone for help. He never would have acknowledged that there was more to life than the riches and comforts he'd relied upon to make him happy.

He had a new family who wanted to know him, and he wanted to know them. He rested his head on the top of Melinda's and choked back his tears as he softly thanked her for not giving up on him.

Finally, Melinda released him and looked up at his face. She smiled and said, "Please, George, come in. We have so much catching up to do."

Epilogue

The investigation into the disappearance of the directors' accounts continued. All of the evidence still indicated that someone from within, or with connections to an insider, had hacked into the private accounts. George Maxwell was eventually cleared of any wrong doing, but he declined Global Financial's offer for him to return to work. The bank had replaced all of the missing funds to the thirteen men, and Global vowed to find the thief at any cost.

Ever since June 6, 2006, George's life as he knew it had been changed irrevocably. He'd had the VeriChip removed from his wrist. He had concerns that he might be condemned already just for taking it. Melinda assured him that the chip itself probably wasn't the actual mark of the Beast because George hadn't vowed an allegiance or worshiped a deity associated with the chip. Even so, he thought of the old prophet's warnings and believed the mark of the Beast was coming. The VeriChip was just one more method to usher it in and to lull the public into accepting a cashless commerce system. George didn't want to take any chances.

Melinda and Richard Andrews told their other two children about Melinda's past and George's adoption when she was fifteen. It was quite a shock to them at first, but they saw how happy their mother was to have George back in her life, and they enjoyed getting to know him also. They eventually understood why Melinda had been so persistent with her crusade against the VeriChip. Even Sarah promised she'd refuse to take it after realizing its dangers and recognizing the divine intervention that had occurred in their lives over the past year.

George's unique knowledge about the world of finance put him in a position to warn others about using biometrics as personal identifiers. He felt responsible for all of the people who had followed his example and had taken the embedded chip. He vowed to try to convince them to reverse their actions as he had. George's knowledge about being exalted and then brought low also helped him to warn others about avoiding the same pitfall.

George Maxwell had been a man of power, and he recognized power when he saw it. He'd come to realize that there was a power that was greater than himself and far beyond his control. He'd thought a lot about that lightning bolt that had dropped out of the sky and missed him only by a foot. If it was sent to get his attention, it had.

He knew that he was blessed with a good mind, a good education, and unlimited energy. He knew he'd be OK.

George realized that God had heard his prayers at St. Paul's Chapel that day. He recalled how he had quickly rattled off his petitions and fired a lot of questions to God about what he should or shouldn't do. But then he got up and left and went back to his office and buried himself in his work. He never took the time to be still and listen and wait for God to answer.

George wanted to take Melinda to St. Paul's Chapel one day soon and share it with her. He wanted to tell her about its history and about the day he went there and prayed for answers before the event at Federal Hall. On his next visit, he would be going with a thankful heart. The next time he would sit for a while and be still and take the time to listen. The next time he wouldn't be alone.

To order additional copies of

Have your credit card ready and call

Toll free: (877) 421-READ (7323)

or order online at: www.winepressbooks.com